The Siege of Durgam's Folly

Author: Mike Mearls
Appendix C Author: Björn Strohecker
Developers: Clark Peterson and Bill Webb
Project Manager: Zach Glazar
Editor: Jeff Harkness
SW Conversion: Jeff Harkness
Art Direction: Casey Christofferson
Layout and Graphic Design: Charles A. Wright
Cover Design: Charles A. Wright
Cover Art: Josh Stewart
Interior Art: Adrian Landeros and Brian LeBlanc
Cartography: Robert Altbauer
Fantasy Grounds Conversion: Michael G. Potter

©2020 Frog God Games. All rights reserved. Reproduction without the written permission of the publisher is expressly forbidden. Frog God Games and the Frog God Games logo is a trademark of Frog God Games. All characters, names, places, items, art and text herein are copyrighted by Frog God Games, Inc. The mention of or reference to any company or product in these pages is not a challenge to the trademark or copyright concerned.

Product Identity: The following items are hereby identified as Frog God Games LLC's Product Identity, as defined in the Open Game License version 1.0a, Section 1(e), and are not Open Game Content: product and product line names, logos and identifying marks including trade dress; artifacts; creatures; characters; stories, storylines, plots, thematic elements, dialogue, incidents, language, artwork, symbols, designs, depictions, likenesses, formats, poses, concepts, themes and graphic, photographic and other visual or audio representations; names and descriptions of characters, spells, enchantments, personalities, teams, personas, likenesses and special abilities; places, locations, environments, creatures, equipment, magical or supernatural abilities or effects, logos, symbols, or graphic designs; and any other trademark or registered trademark clearly identified as Product Identity. Previously released Open Game Content is excluded from the above list.

Frog God Games is:

Bill Webb, Matthew J. Finch, Zach Glazar, Charles A. Wright, Edwin Nagy, Mike Badolato, John Barnhouse

FROG GOD GAMES
ISBN: 978-1-62283-877-6

Table of Contents

INTRODUCTION

The Siege of Durgam's Folly is an adventure for four to six characters of 4th- to 6th-level. Smaller parties or parties with fewer combat-oriented characters should rely either on diplomacy and stealth or be higher level to be successful. You can tailor the number of ogres at the fort to fit the required challenge level for the players.

ADVENTURE BACKGROUND

Durgam's Folly has long stood guard on the frontier between civilized lands and the chaotic wilderness. Originally founded ages ago by the famous military captain Durgam Volmsmer, the fortress was disdained by many who said it would never stand, that it would quickly succumb to the evil creatures of the surrounding wilds. Though the fortress was a constant target of orc and goblin attacks, with each successive victory the forces of man drove the encroaching humanoids farther and farther into the wilderness. It is now said that Durgam's Folly is unconquerable, proof against any external threat.

Unfortunately, while the fort has repulsed all attackers, it is not, as its guardians recently found out, immune to internal treachery.

Theodocious the Forger is a powerful wizard known for his unmatched skill in creating and devising new magical formulae. Not only is his workmanship unparalleled, but his ingenious application of magical principles in creating new items has earned him an important position in the royal court, that of chief artificer. Theodocious has been charged by the king to devise innovative magical defenses for the kingdom. To this end, Theodocious set up a magical workshop at Durgam's Folly, both to escape the prying eyes of the kingdom's rivals and to work in an environment where he could gain a firsthand glimpse into the workings and needs of the king's army.

Soon after arriving at Durgam's Folly, Theodocious hit upon a brilliant scheme. While golems are powerful, the cost and work needed to build them make fielding the constructs in an army prohibitive. Instead, Theodocious went to work on building a new type of golem, the clockwork colony. This magical construct is made up of a horde of tiny golems. Individually, these golems are hardly more powerful than a bug. When working together, however, the golems can combine to form powerful fighting units. Furthermore, the golems are adaptable, capable of modifying their colony unit to react and adjust to changing conditions. Each clockwork colony is guided by a single communal intelligence centered on a brain gear that receives orders from a human master and directs the colony accordingly.

Theodocious' creation was a success. Unfortunately, it proved too successful. Soon after the wizard created his first clockwork colony, the brain gear achieved self-awareness. Following up on the military doctrine and tactical guidelines dictated to it, the colony overwhelmed the fort's garrison while it slept and took many soldiers prisoner, including Theodocious. The colony has claimed the fortress as its lair, and even now the brain gear has dispatched scouts to reconnoiter the surrounding countryside and select the next target for an attack.

Little did Theodocious know that deep within the crypts beneath Durgam's Folly there lurked an ancient evil. Years ago, the original builders of Durgam's Folly chose the fort's site because of the ruined structure that stood there, giving them a head start on construction and providing them with at least some fortification to rely on as they worked to raise the fort. The builders never suspected that the ruins were once a temple dedicated to dark and blasphemous gods. As Theodocious used his magic to expand the cellars where he pursued his research beneath the fort, he eventually opened a passage to the long-sealed inner sanctum of the dark temple. It was at this time that the brain gear, influenced by the sudden influx of dark magic, achieved sentience.

The brain gear now claims Theodocious as its thrall. The wizard has been forced into servitude, working to develop and build new clockwork creations to serve the brain gear's limitless ambition.

The fort's commanders have also been subjected to the brain gear's gruesome experiments, leaving them hollow shells that now also serve the awakened machine. The surviving members of the garrison, imprisoned by the brain gear's clockwork followers, are kept around as possible slave laborers or test subjects for some of the brain gear's more insidious inventions. Not content to merely sit back and let the situation develop, the brain gear used its mystic powers to contact a cunning ogre named Grimulak. At the brain gear's prodding, the ogre rallied the ogres who inhabit the wilderness around Durgam's Folly to his banner. The brain gear has learned from Theodocious that a supply caravan is due back at the fort any day now. The brain gear feels somewhat vulnerable to attack and sees the ogres as a temporary, though useful, ally. Once the brain gear, with the help of Theodocious, constructs a legion of powerful clockwork creations, it plans to aggressively carve out a realm for itself from the surrounding region.

The brain gear is not driven by simple greed or lust for power. As noted above, it gained sentience due to the influence of a dark power long hidden beneath Durgam's Folly. While the brain gear is not aware of it, a major part of its personality is influenced by the long-forgotten dark cult that riled the region around the fort many years ago. The brain gear is an unwitting servant of Orcus, the dark lord of the undead. The demon lord finds the current situation somewhat intriguing. Should the brain gear enjoy any level of success, Orcus plans on contacting the construct and turning it to his cause. To this end, Orcus dispatched some minor demonic entities to watch over and aid the brain gear. To Orcus' amusement and his minions' dismay, the brain gear reacted to the sudden appearance of demons within the fort by launching an aggressive attack against them. The battle destroyed many of the brain gear's clockwork creations. Its defenses weakened, the brain gear's position is currently somewhat precarious. While the ogres under the control of Grimulak now man the fort against any intruders, the brain gear puts little faith in them. It originally wanted them only as test subjects, viewing them as far too unreliable to ever be trustworthy and useful minions. The brain gear, after so easily overwhelming the fort garrison, feels it has little to fear from the weak and pathetic humans who could not stand against it and thus does not feel the need to fortify its defenses before delving further into its work to create more powerful clockworks.

NOTES

The Siege of Durgam's Folly is divided into three acts. In the first act, the characters travel across the wilderness to Durgam's Folly while guarding a shipment of expensive and rare spell components for the master wizard Theodocious. This section of the adventure requires the characters to practice diplomacy in winning the trust of their fellow caravan guards and, in a glimpse of things to come, thrusts them into the role of military commanders who must use tactical planning to overcome a motivated and intelligent enemy.

The second part of the adventure covers the characters' arrival at Durgam's Folly, which they find under the control of a band of barbaric ogres. Using stealth and superior tactics, the characters must infiltrate the fortress and overwhelm the ogres before they can mount a successful defense. If the characters attempt a frontal assault, they may find the ogres too strong to defeat.

In the final act, the characters learn that the brain gear, a self-aware magical construct, is behind toppling the fort and the rise of the ogre horde. The characters must descend into the cellars and dungeons beneath the fort and destroy the brain gear once and for all. The brain gear, as its name indicates, is a cunning foe that sets a series of deadly traps, fearsome guardians, and other obstacles in front of the characters. Once the characters overcome these obstacles, they must journey into the ancient temple's inner sanctum and destroy the dark creatures that Theodocious accidentally awakened. Only then can they destroy the brain gear and the threat it poses to civilization.

This adventure requires the characters to tackle a variety of roleplaying challenges. Sound tactical thinking, careful negotiating, alert roleplaying, and clever problem solving are all necessary to carry the day. Remember that the villains presented in this adventure are brilliant minds who used their intelligence — not their sword arms — to assume their positions of power. Don't sell them short and play them as unthinking or dumb brutes. If you see the chance to improvise a cunning plan on their behalf, go for it.

ADAPTING THE ADVENTURE

As described within the adventure, Durgam's Folly stands at the edge of civilization within the Stoneheart Mountains. However, you should be able to radically change the setting and nature of the fort without requiring too much modification to the plot, as most of the action takes place within or beneath the fort. The journey to the fort requires some modification if you move Durgam's Folly to a desert, an arctic, or some other exotic locale. The critical trait that you should preserve in placing Durgam's Folly in your game world is the fort's isolation from civilization. The brain gear's mutiny should occur in relative secrecy, allowing it to plan its next moves over the course of a few weeks and leaving it well prepared to deal with the characters. If Durgam's Folly stands very close to a city or along a major trade route, chances are that someone discovers something amiss before the characters arrive. Be prepared to offer up an explanation for this if you want to drop Durgam's Folly along a heavily-traveled road or in a populous region.

ADVENTURE HOOKS

You can involve a group of characters in the adventure in several ways. The introduction assumes that the party travels to Durgam's Folly with a caravan bearing tools and supplies for Theodocious. The easiest plot hooks involve the characters' hiring on to escort the caravan. However, this is sometimes easier said than done. Ideally, if the characters do not journey with the caravan to Durgam's Folly, you can still work with various creatures in the adventure, as they help provide clues about the current situation at the fort and help build a sense of dread and isolation in the players.

You might choose to have the characters present for the initial attack by the brain gear. In this case, you have to wing most of the details yourself, but the included description of the fort, the ogres, and the brain gear should give you enough material to work from without requiring too much improvisation. This option works best if you decide to use Durgam's Folly as a base of operations for several adventures in your campaign. The characters could journey there, meet Theodocious, engage in a few expeditions into the wilds around the fort, and then deal with the menace posed by the brain gear.

The following adventure hooks are provided to give you a reasonable explanation why the characters have chosen to journey to Durgam's Folly. If you are planning out a campaign, the hooks might give you some ideas on how to work this adventure into your story without disrupting the flow of your game or causing an abrupt shift from one storyline to another.

• The local government hires the characters for the princely sum of 2,000 gp each to guard a simple merchant caravan. The characters' contract explains that the caravan bears some rare and valuable alchemical mixtures that must arrive safely at the fort. Thus, experts such as the characters are needed to ensure the shipment's safety.

• Theodocious, eager to field-test his new creations, contacts the characters with a business proposition. He wishes for an adventuring band to take a few of his creations on an expedition to a nearby dungeon in hopes of testing his creations in a combat situation. He wishes to meet the characters at Durgam's Folly and offers to pay them 500 gp each just for showing up to hear his plan. Luckily for the characters, a supply caravan is leaving for Durgam's Folly the same day as they are. Theodocious dares not mention his works in the letter for fear of attracting spies, but he does hint that the characters will have a chance to render a great service to those in power, people who are sure to remember the characters' deeds in the future.

• A rival of Theodocious hires the characters to journey to Durgam's Folly, observe the master artificer at work, and then report back all they learn. The characters' patron arranges for the characters to journey to the fort under the guise of caravan guards hired to escort the latest shipment of the fort's supplies.

• The characters discover a magical item or need advice concerning some arcane matter. They consult several sages but learn that only Theodocious the Forger, who is currently living at Durgam's Folly, has the knowledge they seek. A caravan is forming to head for the fort, and if the characters are willing, the caravan master is more than happy to hire them on as guards.

• While journeying across the wilderness, the characters come across a large band of ogres attacking a caravan. Many of the caravan guards are dead, and the ogres are preparing to launch an assault that should destroy the last of the caravan's defenders. If the characters step into the fray, they easily drive away the ogres. As it turns out, this is a caravan bound for Durgam's Folly. Its surviving members beg the characters to accompany them to the fort.

• A ranger or druid receives word from his woodland allies that a great horde of ogres is gathering to assault Durgam's Folly. The characters must journey to the fort and warn the garrison. According to the character's contact, lately guard patrols from the fort have ceased to marshal out into the wilderness, thus allowing humanoids and bandits to operate unopposed.

Act I: The Journey to Durgam's Folly

This portion of the adventure assumes that the characters elect to journey with a caravan to Durgam's Folly. However, should the characters elect to make the journey on their own, or if you decide to use some other method to bring the characters to the fort, each encounter in this section includes notes for adapting to situations that do not involve the caravan.

The Caravan

Trina, a wizard and apprentice to Theodocious, leads the group heading to Durgam's Folly. She commands 20 guards, two sergeants named Thevik and Uli, and eight wagons, each of which is pulled by two horses. Unfortunately for Trina, she hasn't had the time or money to hire any more guards. The warriors with the caravan are all members of the Durgam's Folly garrison, and while the fort commander, Captain Evrik, was ordered to provide maximum support to Theodocious, neither he nor the wizard was willing to strip the garrison to guard the caravan.

Trina is quite the pessimist, and she managed to convince Theodocious to set aside 800 gp for her to hire additional swordsmen to help watch over the caravan. But sadly, she has no money to offer prospective warriors up front, leaving her with no mercenaries willing to enter her service. Should the characters approach her with an offer to help guard the caravan, she gladly accepts, promising them 800 gp once they arrive at the fort.

Caravan Personnel

Trina, as noted above, is an ardent pessimist. She assumes that what can go wrong will go wrong and is not afraid to let others know she feels that way. However, unlike many pessimists, Trina takes an active role in preparing for the misfortunes that she sees as inevitable. A relentless planner and organizer, she attacks the task of leading the caravan with an almost fanatical abandon. She takes the role of a military field commander, happily inserting herself above the soldiers and often micromanaging the details of guarding the caravan. Theodocious set her to this task partly to get the girl out of his hair, yet he also knows that she of all his apprentices has the attention to detail and keen mind for planning to successfully complete the task. Trina expects the characters to toe the line and obey her orders, but she is by no means a tyrant or fool. While she may dog them with questions about the watch rotation they just arranged, grill them on their tactical experience, and pester them into delivering regular and detailed reports on the status and morale of the guards, she above all else wants the caravan journey to go as smoothly as possible. She's more than willing to listen to someone else's plan, but her analytical mind and keen attention to detail drive her to thoroughly question and debate any ideas.

Trina stands five feet five inches tall, and has long, flowing brown hair streaked with gray despite the fact that she's only 25. Her face is plain and often marked with a deep scowl or a look of deep thought. She prefers simple traveling clothes to robes or other impractical clothing. She speaks in direct terms, disdaining flowery speech or tact in favor of efficiency. Her raven familiar, **Croaker**, often perches on her shoulder. Croaker is most definitely his master's familiar, echoing her pessimism tenfold and reinforcing it with his sarcastic attitude.

Thevik and **Uli** are both veteran warriors in Durgam's Folly's garrison. Thevik is in her mid-30s, with short, close-cropped blonde hair and a wiry, six-foot-one-inch frame. Her stern and businesslike manner instantly won Trina's respect. The guards also deeply respect her, as she worked her way from buck private to sergeant through hard work, grit, and determination. Thevik expects the best from her men, and her fair manner and natural toughness go a long way toward getting it from them.

Uli is a large man bordering on obese. He has dark, curly hair and sports four days' worth of stubble on his face. Unlike Thevik, Uli is looked down on as a bully and braggart by the guards. While a skilled warrior, he relies on shouted threats to push the men into action. Uli is also a bit of a chauvinist and often chafes under the command of Trina (who is unworthy to command in his eyes, since she isn't a soldier) and Thevik (whom he is jealous of both for her success and the respect the men show her).

The **guards** are all professional soldiers who work hard to obey orders to the best of their ability. They were chosen for this task precisely for their skill and dedication and look at this extended duty away from their base as a chance to prove themselves as capable soldiers.

The Journey to Durgam's Folly

The trip to the fort takes three days for the caravan wagons, as the fort is roughly 55 miles away from the frontier. The caravan leaves at sunrise and spends three days and nights on the road, arriving at the fort at late morning of the fourth day. Optionally, you could easily extend this journey if you wish to start the adventure somewhere farther within the heartland of civilization. Trina was sent to gather supplies and tools for Theodocious, after all, and such an errand may require her to journey to a large city to fill her master's request. Feel free to fill out the journey with extra encounters. The encounters outlined below assume that the party has passed beyond the frontier and is within three days of Durgam's Folly. If the characters travel at a faster or slower pace than the average 16 miles per day for a wagon, adjust the timing and/or location of the encounters accordingly.

Unless the characters convince her otherwise, Trina stations guards in columns along the caravan's flank. One guard drives each wagon, while the rest of the guards ride on horses. If the characters do not have horses, Trina arranges for riding horses for any who need them. At night, Trina breaks the guards into three watches of seven, seven, and six guards each (the characters are free to join whichever watch they think is best, though Trina has her suggestions). Uli sits up with the first watch, Thevik with the middle one, and Trina with the last one. Trina insists that the characters each take a watch, ideally spreading themselves out across the three watches. She arranges the wagons in a rough circle, with the horses and sleeping guardsmen in the middle and those on watch walking the perimeter.

Trina, Female Human (MU4): HP 10; **AC** 7[12] or 2[17] (missile) and 4[15] (melee) from *shield* spell; **Atk** staff (1d6); **Move** 12; **Save** 10 (+2, ring); **AL** N; **CL/XP** 4/120; **Special:** +2 saves vs. spells, spells (3/2).

Spells: 1st—*light, magic missile, shield*; 2nd—*invisibility, phantasmal force.*

Equipment: traveling clothes, staff, *+2 ring of protection*, scroll (*magic missile, read magic, web*).

Croaker the Raven: HD 1d4hp; **HP** 3; **AC** 6[13]; **Atk** bite (1d2); **Move** 2 (fly 12); **Save** 18; **AL** N; **CL/XP** A/5; **Special:** none. (*Monstrosities* 387)

Thevik, Female Human (Ftr2): HP 13; **AC** 5[14]; **Atk** longsword (1d8) or spear (1d6) or longbow x2 (1d6); **Move** 12; **Save** 13; **AL** N; **CL/XP** 2/30; **Special:** multiple attacks (2) vs. creatures with 1 or fewer HD.
Equipment: chainmail, longsword, spear, longbow, 20 arrows, 2d4 sp.

Uli, Male Human (Ftr2): HP 10; **AC** 5[14]; **Atk** longsword (1d8) or spear (1d6) or light crossbow (1d4+1); **Move** 9; **Save** 13; **AL** N; **CL/XP** 2/30; **Special:** multiple attacks (2) vs. creatures with 1 or fewer HD.
Equipment: chainmail, longsword, spear, light crossbow, 20 bolts.

Caravan Guards, Male or Female Human Warriors (20): HD 1; **HP** 8x3, 7x5, 6x8, 5x2, 4x2; **AC** 6[13]; **Atk** longsword (1d8) or light crossbow (1d4+1); **Move** 12; **Save** 17; **AL** N; **CL/XP** 1/15; **Special:** none. (*Monstrosities* 257)
Equipment: leather armor, shield, longsword, light crossbow, 20 bolts.

ENCOUNTER 1:
THE RUINS OF HANSONBURG

Ahead stands the small village of Hansonburg. The village is a welcome sight on the dull road, as it holds the promise of a freshly made bed, hot food, and a mug of fine ale. The caravan guards brighten visibly as word spreads up and down the line of wagons that the town is in sight. As the characters draw closer, the promise of comfort turns to one of tension and fear. No lights shine in the windows of the village's buildings, and none walk among the settlements. Surely at this time of day the inn at the center of the tiny settlement would be alive with activity. But as they draw nearer, the stark silence surrounding the settlement grows more ominous.

Hansonburg is a tiny thorp roughly halfway between Durgam's Folly and the last major outpost of civilization. The caravan, if it proceeds at a normal rate, arrives there at sundown.

Two nights ago, a group of ogres led by Grimulak silently crept up on Hansonburg and murdered every last one of its inhabitants. Using his *invisibility* and *polymorph self* abilities, Grimulak easily disposed of the guards before leading the ogres into town. Under the Grimulak's iron-fisted command, the ogres methodically moved from house to house, killing the inhabitants in their sleep and quickly running down and killing those who tried to escape.

Searching the town turns up little of note. The attackers obviously met with little struggle, as there are few signs of conflict. Characters may note a large number of ogre tracks heading into the town from the south and leaving to the north. While the tracks are often confusing in many places where they crisscross repeatedly as the ogres moved through the town, it is obvious that the creatures surrounded the town and systematically eliminated Hansonburg's inhabitants. A search of the houses and inn reveals that no foodstuff or drink remains in any building, and all of the buildings are in extreme disarray, as if they were thoroughly searched and looted. Grimulak led the ogres here to raid the settlement for supplies, hoping to stockpile enough food

and other necessities to let his horde survive for some time without hunting. In addition, Grimulak struck knowing that the garrison at Durgam's Folly is out of commission, allowing him to attack without fear of reprisal.

The ogres are long since gone, as they continued on their journey to assemble with the other tribes soon after completing their foul deeds here. No bodies remain — the ogres carried them off to stock their larders. Emphasize the eerie silence and sharp contrast between the once vibrant community and its now-empty shell. From the outside, the buildings are largely undamaged, and few signs of conflict are readily apparent to the casual observer. Most of the houses' doors hang open, though, and inside the houses are many signs of violence: bloodstained sheets and beds, ransacked rooms, signs of forced entry, and even a few places where a quick, pitched fight may have taken place. If asked, the caravan guards admit that Hansonburg's militia was composed primarily of farmers barely trained in the use of a sword who alternated taking night watches. Being so close to Durgam's Folly, the town depended on the garrison for its defense. The guards assume that a patrol from the fort must have been through the town recently, though there are not any horse tracks or signs of human footprints coming from or heading to the fort.

The caravan guards are particularly hard hit by the ruins of the town, as many of them had at least a passing acquaintance with the villagers. Trina is severely unnerved by the ruins and urges the caravan to move forward and away from the town. She insists on doubling the guard at night and demands that anyone who does not need to rest to prepare spells get by on only four hours of sleep. Somewhat sheltered as an apprentice, she turns to the characters for advice on what may have been behind the raid and what she can do to ensure the caravan's safety. The atmosphere surrounding the caravan becomes much tenser. Uli takes his fear and worries out on his men, verbally abusing them and loudly boasting that he'll personally lead a patrol to track down whoever was responsible for the attack. He volunteers to take the point duty. Thevik takes care to keep a close eye on her men and, if possible, makes a point of speaking to the characters and Trina about the situation. She knows that ogres, trolls, giants, and orcs have been active in the area in the past but has never seen anything quite so bold as an attack on a settlement. Attacks on small groups of travelers or caravans are not uncommon, but the last full-scale attack on a settlement took place more than 20 years ago.

ENCOUNTER 2: OGRES

This encounter takes place at noon the day after the characters leave Hansonburg. Read or paraphrase the following, depending on how the caravan guards are arranged and where the characters ride relative to the wagons and other guards. The description assumes that Uli is at the head of the caravan, riding point with a few other soldiers.

After yesterday's gruesome discovery, a black cloud has descended upon the entire caravan. The guards cast wary glances at the trees beside the road, ready for an assault to strike at any moment. What was once a simple, almost leisurely journey has become an ordeal, heavy with unease and fear. The tension of the journey is shattered by shouts from up ahead. A guard under Uli's command at the front of the caravan gallops toward you, shouting that Uli has tracked down an ogre responsible for the sacking of Hansonburg.

An **ogre** who had taken part in the raid is indeed on the road up ahead. During the attack, he and a few of his comrades hid several kegs of ale looted from the village in the nearby woods. Two nights ago, they returned for their stash and immediately began to indulge in it. Graulg, in particular, overindulged to an incredible degree even

for an ogre and spent the past two nights sleeping in a ditch. If the characters rush up to the front of the caravan, they discover Uli and five of the guards with crossbows trained on the thing. The ogre sits on the side of the road, cradling his head and moaning piteously. Unless the characters intercede, Uli and the guards kill him with a volley of crossbow bolts. The sergeant has his crossbow pointed against the ogre's throat; if fired, this kills the ogre outright.

To convince Uli to spare the ogre's life, the characters must somehow persuade him to stand down. Uli is consumed with bloodlust and is eager to avenge the destruction of Hansonburg, as are the guards. The characters face a decidedly uphill battle in talking the guard sergeant down from his rage. If the characters appeal to his sense of pity or justice, they'll have a much harder time convincing him. Uli considers the ogre less than human and wants only to show it the same mercy it showed the people of Hansonburg. On the other hand, if the characters tell Uli that they wish only to question the thing to bring its comrades to justice, they are much more likely to succeed. Trina and Thevik are torn by their desire for revenge and the need to learn more information, but they are much easier to convince if presented with reasonable explanations of why the ogre should live. If Thevik sides with the characters, the guards begin to waver, but Uli's attitude does not change. While Trina should be able to order Uli to stand down, her doing so only angers the sergeant.

Graulg, Male Ogre: HD 4+1; HP 25; AC 5[14]; Atk club (1d10+1); Move 9; Save 13; AL C; CL/XP 4/120; Special: drunkenness (−1 to hit and saves). (*Monstrosities* 356)

If Uli spares the ogre, the characters can learn the following pieces of information from him (in addition to the information provided about him above). The ogre is still very inebriated and speaks in slow, slurred, and choppy common:

• The ogres have taken control of Durgam's Folly. A few of the tribes are there now, and Graulg and a few other ogres went there to join up with the horde. (True — ever opportunistic, no ogre wants to miss out on the chance for loot should the horde decide to launch a raid on civilized lands.)

• A powerful ogre with magical powers leads the horde. This ogre ordered the raid on Hansonburg. (Partially true — the brain gear suggested the raid, primarily because once word spread that the fort was controlled by ogres, some opportunistic band of evil humanoids would raid the village. The brain gear figured it might as well be the ogres.)

• Grimulak often spends time in the tunnels beneath the fort, speaking with those he calls, "the ones below." These creatures are allies of Grimulak that he has bound with his magic. (False — Grimulak takes orders from the brain gear, but he cannot afford to let the rank-and-file ogres know that or he'll lose face.)

• Life has been great at the castle. By day, the ogres train in fighting under the cruel sign, but at night they carouse, drain the fort's stock of ale and food, and enjoy their conquest (True.)

• Grimulak is blessed by the gods. He can turn invisible and make himself look like other creatures. (True — he often demonstrates his powers to awe new recruits.)

If asked about the other ogres in the area, Graulg claims that they're all at the fort. That's what the ogre thinks. In truth, many ogres are still journeying to the fort to rally beneath Grimulak's banner. The ogre is still inebriated but recovers his wits after eight or more hours of sleep. If penned up in a wagon, he tries his hardest to escape, preferring to flee into the wilderness rather than rejoin his comrades at the fort in shame.

Trina visibly blanches when she receives word that the fort has fallen. She assumes that foreign spies or some evil power received word of Theodocious' work and moved to capture the wizard and his creations. She insists that the caravan continue its journey. She does agree to send a courier back to civilization with word that the fort has fallen, but she refuses to waste time in turning the entire caravan around. While she does not disclose the nature of Theodocious' work, she insists that the characters and the rest of the caravan must get to the fort as soon as possible. The guards do know something about magical experiments taking place at the fort, and if pressed, they admit to the characters that this may be the reason behind Trina's desire to keep moving to the fort.

If the characters volunteer to ride ahead of the rest of the caravan, modify the remaining encounters. The ogre ambush in **Encounter 5** assumes that the characters are with the rest of the caravan. If they are not, reduce the number of ogres to six. The wyvern in **Encounter 3** does not attack the characters, as it thinks its prey is hidden in a wagon, but it more than likely destroys the caravan if it lacks the characters' protection.

ENCOUNTER 3: DEATH FROM ABOVE

This encounter takes place during the night of the second day of travel.

The night is cool and clear. A gentle breeze rustles the trees and runs through your hair, helping to dispel the weariness of the past few days and ease the guards' troubled looks. Above you, the stars twinkle like diamonds spread across black velvet. Suddenly, your view of the night sky is disrupted. You blink your eyes for a moment. Did the stars just disappear for the briefest moment? A thunderous, roaring cry in the sky and the flapping of tremendous wings echoes through the night. The stars didn't disappear — some monstrous creature just flew above you.

Using its powers, the brain gear convinced a **wyvern** that nests in the nearby mountains that wagons passing along the road to the fort are weighed down with tasty delicacies and fresh food. Eager for an easy meal, the wyvern has regularly swooped over the road, looking for the food promised it in its dreams. Unfortunately for the characters, it thinks it just found it.

The guards react with temporary panic. Each round, a character may shout to the frightened men and women to convince 1d4+1 guards to shake off the panic and fight the wyvern. The wyvern first attempts to snatch and throw a wagon. Once it sees that the wagons are empty of food, it attacks mercilessly, fleeing only when reduced to fewer than half of its hit points. The wyvern targets human-sized targets indiscriminately, snatching up guards, characters, or whoever is the easiest target. Characters who take cover under the trees are not subject to attacks from the wyvern. If the entire caravan moves under cover, the wyvern circles the area for two minutes before flying off in search of easier pickings.

Wyvern: HD 8; HP 52; AC 3[16]; Atk bite (2d8) or sting (1d6 + poison); Move 6 (fly 24); Save 8; AL N; CL/XP 10/1400; Special: poison sting (save or die). (*Monstrosities* 519)

ENCOUNTER 4: EYES IN THE NIGHT

This encounter takes place during the early evening of the third day of travel as the characters come within 10 miles of the fort.

Though the guards have been silent for many hours, their strained looks and downcast manner speak volumes of how trying this journey has been. The forest around you is quiet, save for the occasional bird call ahead of you. The woods grow even thicker and crowd closer to the road.

The brain gear, using its overseer clockworks, has dispatched many scouting parties to watch the roads leading to Durgam's Folly. In the woods ahead, **4 clockwork scouts** and a **clockwork overseer** lie hidden in the trees. The scouts are disguised to look like house cats. They lurk among the tree trunks, keeping a careful eye out for any passersby. The overseer hides farther back from the scouts, roughly 60 feet from the road. If the characters specifically scan the trees looking for any threat, they have a 2-in-6 chance to see the scouts. If spotted, the scouts flee back in the direction of the overseer. Remember that the scouts become inactive if they lose contact with the brain gear, which occurs should they move more than 100 feet away from the overseer or if the overseer is destroyed. If the characters discover the scouts and attack, there is a 10% chance per round that the brain gear contacts the overseer and learns of the characters. If the characters destroy the overseer before this happens, then the brain gear learns nothing more than that its minion has been destroyed. Obviously, if the characters do not discover the scouts, the brain gear learns about the approaching caravan.

The clockwork scouts are disguised with the skins from a few cats that the fort garrison kept as pets. It's possible that if a member of the caravan crew spots the scouts first, he or she may mistake them for the fort's cats run astray. If Trina is confronted with the remains of a clockwork, she discloses the nature of Theodocious' work to the characters and admits that she believes attackers struck the fort to claim the wizard's inventions for themselves. She emphasizes that the caravan needs to make it to the fort as soon as possible and hopefully capture the thieves before they can make off with the clockworks. She is also quite afraid for Theodocious and wants nothing unpleasant to happen to her master.

Clockwork Overseer: HD 2; HP 13; AC 2[17]; Atk slam (1d6); **Move** 15; **Save** 16; **AL** N; **CL/XP** 2/30; **Special:** none. (*The Tome of Horrors Complete* 99 or **Appendix B: New Monsters**)

Clockwork Scouts (4): HD 1; HP 8, 6x2, 5; AC 2[17]; **Atk** slam (1d4); **Move** 15; **Save** 17; **AL** N; **CL/XP** 1/15; **Special:** camouflage (1-in-2 chance to notice; 2-in-6 for elves, dwarves and halflings; 3-in-6 for rangers and druids). (*The Tome of Horrors Complete* 100 or **Appendix B: New Monsters**)

ENCOUNTER 5: AMBUSH

This encounter takes place after midnight of the third day. Depending on how **Encounter 4** progressed, the characters may encounter either a prepared band of **8 ogres** sent to intercept the caravan or a small group dispatched to investigate the sudden disappearance of the overseer and its scouts.

In either case, the ogres march down the road, relying on **4 ogres** sent ahead to scout the way. If the caravan is camped out on or near the road, the ogres move to surround it and attack.

Ogres (8): HD 4+1; HP 31, 28, 27, 24x2, 20, 19, 18; AC 5[14]; **Atk** club (1d10+1); **Move** 9; **Save** 13; **AL** C; **CL/XP** 4/120; **Special:** none. (*Monstrosities* 356)

Tactics: While not the smartest humanoid monsters, ogres do possess a natural cunning. Once they discover the caravan, their response depends on the level of activity surrounding it. If the caravan guards or the characters spot them and sound an alarm, the ogres rush ahead to attack, hoping to catch the caravan before it can prepare a defense.

If the ogres approach the caravan unnoticed, they attack in two waves. The ogres split into two groups of four ogres each. The first group stealthily approaches the caravan before attacking, hoping to surprise the guards and quickly overwhelm them. The second group stations itself on the opposite side of the caravan, hoping to catch any guards who flee from the attacking ogres. Once the guards join the first group of ogres in battle, the second group charges in to catch the defenders from behind and crush them.

Note: While the fight might seem overwhelming, be sure to account for the presence of the guards, the sergeants, and Trina, all of whom help the characters against the ogres.

The ogres accept any surrender and gladly lead the characters back to the fort as their captives. Otherwise, the ogres fight until fewer than six of them remain. At that point, they break for the forest. Any surviving ogres flee the area. They'd much rather flee to the countryside than report their failure to Grimulak. If Graulg is with the caravan as a prisoner, the ogres pay him no mind. Should any of the attacking ogres be taken captive, they know little more than Graulg. Refer to **Encounter 2** for a summary of the information the characters can learn.

If the clockwork scouts and overseer from **Encounter 4** survived, they observe the battle and report back to the brain gear. Make a note of this, as it may affect encounters at the fort.

ENCOUNTER 6: ARRIVAL AT THE FORT

As the characters reach the fort, read or paraphrase the following:

Ahead of you stands your destination, Durgam's Folly. The proud structure stands atop a bare hill, a steep slope helping to protect it from any ground attacks. The road winds out of the woods, across 500 feet of open ground, and heads up a narrow escarpment to the fort's front gate. From here, the fort looks unmanned. Nothing moves along the walls, and no sentinels stand before the open gate. A tattered banner flies from the battlements. It hangs limp before catching in a sudden breeze, revealing its symbol as a clawed green hand crushing a human skull.

Durgam's Folly now stands beneath the rule of Grimulak — the green hand crushing a human skull is his device. The first part of the adventure ends here. Now the characters must endeavor to infiltrate the fort and overthrow the foul ogres who have claimed it.

Act II: The Taking of Durgam's Folly

Durgam's Folly has withstood many assaults during its long and storied history. For many years the fort has stood on the borderlands between the savage, monster-infested wilds and the bucolic civilized lands of man. Were it staffed with resolute, brave, and well-trained warriors, the characters would not stand much of a chance of infiltrating its defenses. Luckily for them, the ogres that now rule the fort are lazy, easily distracted, and somewhat dense. While Grimulak initially ruled the overthrown fort with an iron fist, his control over the ogres has slowly diminished. The chaotic ogres are already chafing under the controlling, evil Grimulak. With the long days that have passed since their initial attack, the ogres have grown restless. At first, they trained in fighting during the day, as few of them ventured out under the sun before joining the horde, and Grimulak wanted them ready to fight under all conditions. The ogres hated this training, though, and more than a few deserted. To keep the rest of the horde together, Grimulak has since given the ogres full access to the ale and wine they captured with the fort. Grimulak and the brain gear are well aware that when the alcohol disappears, the ogres' loyalty will disappear with it.

Given the state of affairs, the fort is poorly defended. Grimulak depends on the brain gear's scouts to alert him of any approaching attackers, as outlined in the encounters on the road to the fort. Grimulak is also in a bit of a precarious situation with the ogres. They know nothing of the brain gear, and if they knew that Grimulak was actually taking orders from something more powerful than he, they might revolt. The truth of the matter is that the brain gear wants to experiment on the ogres and eventually integrate them into its forces. Thus, while it promised Grimulak great treasure and loot if he gathered a horde of ogres, the brain gear is really interested only in gathering more test subjects. The brain gear counseled Grimulak to let the ogres run wild so that they remain in the fort long enough for the brain gear to devise an efficient method to convert them into more usable forms. A few of the ogres that supposedly deserted were dragged down to the dungeons beneath the fort and used as test subjects.

General Notes

The doors throughout the fort are thick, cut from stout wood and reinforced with iron bands.

The entire fort shows signs of abuse at the hands of the ogres. The place is filthy: half-rotten food, discarded ale kegs and other garbage litter the place.

Unlike the typical dungeon, the fort is not described with monsters assigned to each location. Instead, the following paragraphs describe the interior of the fort, and the tactics section gives details on how the ogres react to different actions the party may take. In addition, enough information is provided on the ogres' morale and Grimulak's personality for you to improvise should the players pursue some unforeseen course of action (as they almost invariably do at least once per gaming session!)

Keyed Encounter Areas

The following locations within the fort are keyed to the locations marked on the fort map:

1. Outer Structure

The fort's outer walls are five-foot-thick structures made of stone that stand 15 feet high. A large, wooden gate — the only entrance to the fort — stands open as the characters approach it. The ogres have long since given up defending the gate. The fort itself stands atop a short, flat hill that sharply rises 30 feet. A narrow trail, just wide enough for wagons to navigate single file, snakes in front of the fort, slowly rising up to the gate. The trees and brush in a 500-foot radius around the fort have been cleared out, giving its defenders a clear view of approaching threats.

2. Gatehouse

The gatehouse stands directly above the main gate. The two doors heading into it lead to staircases that spiral up to a long, wide chamber. This room has arrow slits overlooking the approach to the front gate and murder holes in its floor that allow archers to rain arrows and burning oil down on those making their way through the gate. Ladders from this room lead up to the battlements atop the gatehouse.

3. Courtyard

The grass that once covered this courtyard has long since been trampled to plain dirt by the footfalls of countless soldiers, warhorses, and other defenders of the fort.

The ogres lounge outside here during the day if this adventure takes place during summer, spring, or fall, basking in the sun, wrestling each other for fun and sport, or practicing their combat skills.

4. Guard Tower

Each of the towers at the fort's corner stands 30 feet tall and has three floors. The first floor is given over to storage, with weapons, armor, and shields once neatly stacked on shelves, arranged in racks, or hanging from wall pegs. The ogres ransacked each of these storage areas, leaving them chaotic messes, but many usable pieces of equipment remain. Characters can find 2d6 suits of leather armor, 1d6 suits of chainmail, 2d4 large wooden shields, and 2d4 each of longswords, light crossbows, spears, and daggers. Assume the maximum number possible of each type is indeed present, but the difference between the dice results and the maximum represents equipment damaged or destroyed by the ogres.

The second floor, accessible by a staircase from the first, is a barracks. Twenty bunk beds, each flanked by a pair of chests, are neatly arranged along the perimeter of the room. Many of the beds show signs of violence — bloodied sheets, torn feather mattresses — as most of the garrison was overwhelmed in its sleep when the brain gear struck. A long table and several chairs are set in the middle of the room. The ogres have dragged the bedding from the barracks for their own use, but most of the furniture is intact. The stairs from the first floor continue up to the third floor.

The third floor has doors that allow access to the battlements and has arrow slits set into the walls that face areas outside the fort. Quivers of crossbow bolts hang from walls near the slits, 2d4 in total, each holding 20 bolts. The stairs from the second floor continue up to the roof.

A catapult stands atop each tower. While the ogres long since fired off the ammunition to help pass the time, the catapults are all still in working order.

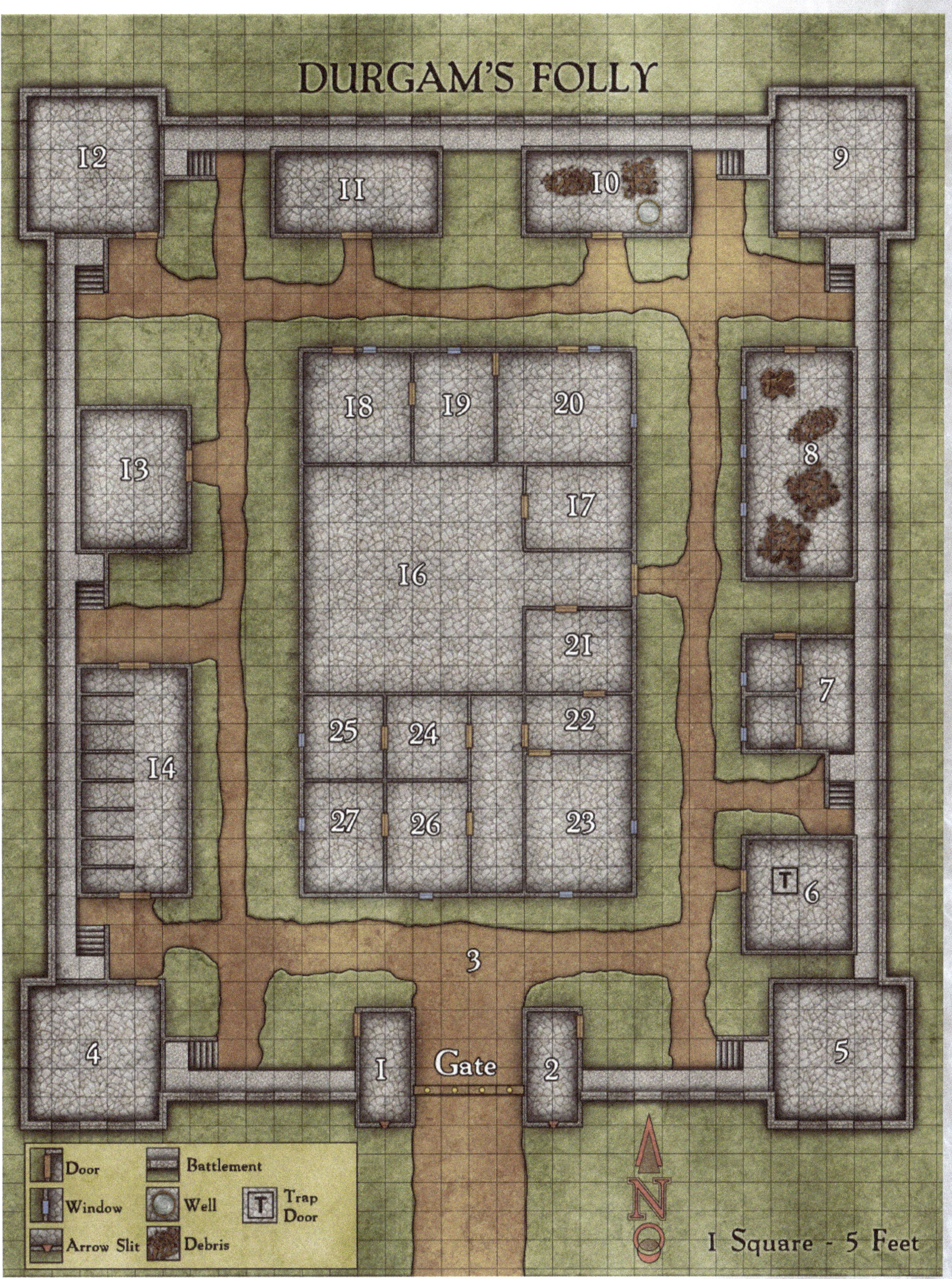

DURGAM'S FOLLY
12
11
10
9
18
19
20
13
8
17
16
7
21
25
24
22
14
27
26
23
6
T
3
4
1
Gate
2
5
Door
Battlement
Window
Well
Trap Door
T
Arrow Slit
Debris
N
1 Square - 5 Feet

5. Guard Tower

This structure is identical in all respects to the building described in **Area 4**.

6. Guard House

This squat, windowless structure is made of the same stone used to build the outer wall. Its door hangs open, revealing a room lined with individual jail cells, all of which currently stand open.

Grimulak holds the keys, and should any characters fall captive to the ogres, they are imprisoned here. In the center of the room is a trapdoor that leads down to the dungeon level detailed in **Act III**. Unlike the prison cells, the trapdoor is kept shut and is securely locked. Picking the lock is more difficult than its shabby looks indicate (–10% Open Locks), as the dungeon below was used to house truly dangerous monsters and criminals with magical abilities. Grimulak holds the key to the trapdoor and often goes below to consult with the brain gear.

7. Theodocious' Quarters

This wooden structure looks somewhat out of place within the fort, as it appears to be a small home that someone rather recently constructed here. The building was once whitewashed, but dirt and filth now cover it. Three windows are set into the building, all of which have been smashed.

This was the private residence of Theodocious, who rested here when he was not working in the dungeons below. The entry room was a sitting room where he entertained visitors and often held discussions with his apprentices. The larger of the two inner rooms was his study, while the small room was his bedroom. The building has been completely emptied of all furniture and other items. Other than the broken windows, the ogres have inflicted no damage to the building. The brain gear ordered this place stripped clean soon after it seized power, as it was eager to learn as much as possible about the process Theodocious used to create it and did not want to leave any evidence undiscovered. The ogres find this place somewhat creepy, and per the brain gear's suggestion, Grimulak ordered them to stay away from it.

8. Chapel

This long, stone building is obviously a chapel. Stained-glass windows, all of which have been smashed, dominated the interior side of the building. Above the large, wooden double doors is a holy symbol for Mithras, god of war.

The interior of the chapel withstood some of the worst abuse meted out by the invading ogre horde. The altar was toppled over, the pews smashed or flipped on their sides. Any character that directly helps restore the altar receives a blessing from the gods in the form of a +1 bonus on their next saving throw. Pushing the altar back to its proper position requires a combined 20 strength.

9. Guard Tower

This tower is much like the tower described in **Area 4**, with one important difference. The **14 guards** taken captive when the brain gear conquered the fort are kept locked in the first floor of this tower. The staircase to the second floor is barricaded with beds and other furniture piled within it by the ogres. The prisoners are kept chained in irons. If rescued, they offer the following information and otherwise help the characters in any way possible, fighting to the death to reclaim the fort. Grimulak has the keys to their irons, or the locks can be picked with thieves' tools.

The guards know:

• Theodocious was working on some sort of golem-like creatures that ran loose and conquered the fort. The creatures struck without warning, and many of the guards were overwhelmed in their sleep.

• Soon after that battle, the ogres arrived and took over the fort.

• Originally, more than 30 guards were kept here, but the ogres regularly come by to drag away a captive, usually choosing someone when they bring the prisoners food and water.

• The guards have no information about the dungeons beneath the fort, as Theodocious allowed no one to enter them without his express permission.

Human Guards (14): HD 1; **AC** 7[12]; **Atk** weapon (1d8); **Move** 12; **Save** 17; **AL** N; **CL/XP** 1/15; **Special:** none. (*Monstrosities* 257)
Note: All of the guards are unarmed and currently have 1d4 hit points.

10. Storage

This long but narrow stone building has seen better days. Its wide, double doors have been torn down, leaving its interior exposed to the elements. Bales of hay, crates, and boxes are scattered about inside of it, as if some powerfully strong toddler rampaged about, tossing everything around in a fit of anger.

The truth behind the state of disarray in this storage building is much simpler. The ogres simply ransacked the place looking for more ale and wine. Having found none, they simply ignored the rest of the items here. There is plenty of food, primarily iron rations. A well stands near the entrance, the pulley, rope, and bucket used to draw water still intact. In addition, horse feed and other supplies were kept here by the garrison. Any character can find any piece of standard, nonmagical equipment worth 5 gp or less in the debris.

11. Storage

Built much like the building next to it, this structure lacks the damage and vandalism committed against its twin. Its doors stand shut, bound with a chain locked against intruders.

Grimulak ordered the ogres to avoid this building, even going as far as to kill one who refused to heed his orders. This storage building holds lumber, nails, bricks, rope, and other materials that Theodocious used in creating the clockworks. The brain gear ordered Grimulak to leave this untouched. Neatly stacked piles of lumber, copper, and iron ingots arranged in neat piles, and boxes of nails, carpentry tools, and metalsmithing implements stand in stark contrast to the disarray of the rest of the fort. The lock on the chain can be opened with thieves' tools and a successful Open Locks check. The chain can also be snapped with a successful Open Doors check with a –1 penalty.

12. Guard Tower

This structure is identical in all details to the building described in **Area 4**.

13. Smithy

The stone structure before you has a large chimney and no windows. The doors leading into it stand open. Within, you can see a forge and bellows. This most likely was the fort's smithy.

As with most of the fort, the ogres long ago ransacked this building for usable items. Interestingly, the smith's tools are all missing. The brain gear ordered Grimulak to haul them all down into the dungeons for its own use in developing its mechanical minions.

14. STABLE

This long, red-painted wooden structure has barn doors set into its north and south sides. Windows, all of which have been smashed, dot the side of the building.

This is the fort's stable. There are enough stalls within to house 20 horses. All of the stalls are now empty, as most of the fort's horses either departed with the caravan or were devoured by the ogres. The floor is covered with hay, and saddles and stirrups for five horses hang from the doors to five of the stalls.

15. INNER KEEP

This large, stone structure is built quite low to the ground, standing barely 10 feet tall. The few windows set into the structure, primarily at its southern end, make the building look more like a prison than the headquarters for a small field army. Iron bars set deep within the walls block the windows. The doors into the building are of the same stout, iron-banded build as the other buildings here. However, these doors are all intact.

All three doors into this building are normally kept locked. The ogres have a simple pass code for entrance: three rapid knocks followed by two heavy knocks spaced two seconds apart. However, the ogre guards at **Area 20** have grown lazy and left the entrance to that room unlocked and unbarred after growing annoyed with constantly opening the door for their comrades. If the characters attempt to enter through a window, they probably have to break the iron bars installed there.

16. FEST HALL

This 40-foot-by-40-foot square room is dominated by three large tables arranged parallel to each other and surrounded with stools and chairs. A fireplace set in the middle of the western wall provides a dim, shadowy glow by which you can see smashed ale kegs piled in the southwest corner and two tapped kegs standing on the middle long table. The entire place smells as if a large number of wild animals have been sleeping here. The filthy furs and blankets spread across the room in small piles confirm that the ogres have used this room as a barracks.

Before the fort fell, this room was used as a dining room, fest hall, and meeting chamber. Currently, the ogres spend the vast majority of their time in here drinking ale, eating, and waiting for something interesting to happen. Searching through the furs scattered about the floors reveals a total of 1,500 gp hidden among the furs in small sacks and belt pouches.

17. STORAGE ROOM

This plain stone room looks as if it once held many kegs of ale, judging by the patterns of dust on the floor and walls. Four kegs stand clustered in the southeast corner of the room.

This room was used as a storage area. The ogres have gone through most of the supplies that were kept here.

18. KITCHEN

A large fireplace on the western wall dominates this room. A black iron cooking pot knocked on its side lies in front of the fireplace. What looks like soup or stew still drips from the pot, adding to the wet mess of vegetables, meat, and dirt that covers the floor. Wooden tables are set along the northern and southern walls, and cooking implements such as knives, forks, and pots are scattered haphazardly across them.

Anyone fighting in this room must make a saving throw each round or fall as the wet floor is quite slick, leading to unsteady and dangerous footing. Treat any cooking implements used in combat as daggers.

19. PANTRY

The ogres found the cured meat from the garrison's latest hunt not to their liking and left it in here to rot. This room is now infested with cockroaches and flies, and the odor is nearly unbearable, though not bad enough to impose any penalties to characters moving through here. The ogres care little for the mess and don't even notice it as they move from room to room.

20. SERVANTS' QUARTERS

This room looks as if it was once a barracks or personal quarters. The four bunk beds in here have been smashed into pieces, the bedding from all of them piled into the southwestern corner. The room has a rank, feral odor to it, as if some large animal has been sleeping in here.

A few ogres, unhappy about the accommodations in **Area 16**, have moved here to sleep. As noted above, the door from this room to the courtyard is not kept locked. Searching through the mess here turns up 200 gp in coins.

21. OFFICE

This was indeed once the office Captain Evrik, the commanding officer of the garrison of Durgam's Folly. The desk has four drawers, all of which have been emptied. A thorough search turns up nothing here, as the brain gear carefully gathered everything in this room, believing that the items may give some insight into human military planning, soon after it seized control of the fort.

22. SITTING ROOM

A soft, red carpet covers the floor of this room, while a silver chandelier set with small candles casts a bright light. Six chairs are arranged in a circle here, with two short tables set between them, and a pair of ottomans set before two of the chairs. Unlike the rest of this place, this room seems somewhat undisturbed.

Grimulak took a liking to this room and wishes to use it in the future, when conferring with whomever else the brain gear recruits for its plans. Thus, he ordered the ogres to stay clear of it.

23. Captain's Bedroom

This large, elegantly appointed bedroom stands in sharp contrast to the ruin and abuse apparent throughout the fort. A large, canopied bed dominates the northeastern corner of the room, while a small writing table stands in the southeast corner. An armoire and a long, standing mirror are against the western wall. The floor here is covered with a soft, blue carpet.

Grimulak claimed this chamber as his own. With his somewhat more civilized sensibilities, unlike the ogres he chose not to destroy the furniture and relieve himself on the floor to make this place feel more like home.

A large journal with a worn, leather cover sits on the writing table beside a quill and an inkpot. This is Grimulak's journal. If the characters spend 10 minutes skimming though it, they learn of Grimulak's background. He describes how a voice came to him in his dreams, showing him how to sneak into the fort and make his way to the dungeons below. There he met a great beast of steel and magic, which commanded him to gather a horde of ogres to take control of Durgam's Folly once its defenders were dead. The journal notes that Grimulak hopes to gain more power and authority as "the voice" (as he refers to the brain gear) gathers more followers and power. He also notes that the ogres have grown lazy and bored lately and that the past few times he went below to confer with the voice, it told him only to stay the course and wait for further orders.

Treasure: Tucked beneath the bed is a plain wooden chest that is locked and trapped. Within are four emeralds worth 250 gp each and the following potions: *animal control*, *giant strength*, *healing* (x4), and *levitation*. Grimulak carries the key to the chest and uses the potions if the need arises.

The lock on the chest can be picked with thieves' tools. A creature who opens the chest without removing the trap is stabbed with the **poison needle** and must succeed on a saving throw or suffer 1d6 points of damage and suffer a –1 penalty to hit for an hour.

If the chest is forcibly opened (by smashing and so on), the trap is bypassed, but the *potions* are shattered.

24. Executive Officer's Study

This small room is dominated by a large wooden desk set against the southern wall. A weapons rack set against the northern wall holds two longswords and a spear. The desk drawers hang open, empty of anything.

Much like the captain's study, this place was ransacked by the brain gear's clockworks looking for anything useful to the brain gear as it formulates its plans.

25. Executive Officer's Room

A bed sits against the southern wall of this room, its sheets and mattress torn and bloody. Blood stains the floor here, and a broken longsword lies on the floor beside the bed.

Much like the rest of the garrison, the executive officer was surprised and killed while sleeping, though not without putting up a fight, as his sword indicates. The blade is notched in several places, as if someone swung it against something extraordinarily hard, such as a stone wall. The resident of this room died fighting against the brain gear's stone golem.

26. Chaplain's Study

This room has been thoroughly ransacked and vandalized. A bent and twisted holy symbol to the war god Mithras hangs on the northern wall. Beneath it is the smashed and charred wreckage of a wooden desk. The ceiling here is stained black from smoke, and ashes coat the entire room.

The ogres, in a drunken stupor, decided to burn the contents of this room and **Area 27** to keep themselves amused. Nothing of value survived the fire.

27. Chaplain's Study

From the looks of this room, someone set off a destructive spell in here or hit it with flaming oil. The furniture — a bed, an armoire, and a small table — is little more than charred rubble. The ceiling is black from soot and smoke, while the walls are streaked with black stains from a fire.

As in **Area 26**, the ogres decided to start a blaze in this room a few days ago to help alleviate their boredom.

The Occupants of the Fort

Currently, **30 ogres** and **Grimulak** occupy the fort. The ogres spend the vast majority of their time drinking and carousing in **Area 16**. To many of them, the occupation of the fort has become little more than an ale-soaked holiday. Grimulak claimed **Areas 22** and **23** as his own. He finds the ogres somewhat repugnant and spends most of his time either in his room dreaming up schemes to place himself atop the brain gear's chain of command or in the dungeons beneath the fort consulting with the clockworks that dwell there.

By day, 25 of the ogres sleep in **Area 16**, and another five sleep in **Area 20**. Grimulak spends his days in the dungeons below the fort, usually in **Area 2** (see **Act III** for details on the dungeons). At night, the ogres are much more active. About 15 of them spend their time in **Area 16**, drinking ale, eating food looted from **Area 10**, and entertaining themselves with arm wrestling, smashing furniture, or telling stories. Five more stand watch in **Area 20**, but these fellows usually keep a steady stream of ale coming from **Area 16** and pay the door little mind. Another five usually remain in **Area 17**, discussing among themselves plans for the future of the fort and lording over the remaining stock of ale. Five ogres patrol the courtyard, making regular 10-minute circuits around the fort, while another five man the gatehouse. Grimulak is either in **Area 16** with his troops or by himself in **Area 22** (50% chance of either).

Grimulak, Male Ogre Mage: HD 5+4; HP 38; AC 4[15];
   Atk two-handed sword (1d12) or longbow x2 (1d6); **Move** 12
   (fly 18); **Save** 12; **AL** C; **CL/XP** 7/600; **Special:** regenerate
   (1hp/round), spell-like abilities. (***Monstrosities*** 359)
   Spell-like Abilities: at will—*darkness 15ft radius*,
   invisibility, *polymorph self*; 1/day—*charm person*, cone of
   frost (60ft range, 20ft diameter blast, 8d6 damage to all, save
   for half), *sleep*.
   Equipment: two-handed sword, longbow, 20 arrows, key to
   chest in **Area 23**, *bag of holding* containing 3,000 gp, a silver
   coffer inlaid with gems (1,000 gp), a gold necklace set with a
   small red ruby (750 gp), and a jade figurine of a small dragon
   (250 gp).

Ogres (30): HD 4+1; AC 5[14]; Atk club (1d10+1); **Move** 9;
   Save 13; **AL** C; **CL/XP** 4/120; **Special:** none. (***Monstrosities***
   356)

CHANCE OF OGRES INVESTIGATING NOISES

Ogres have a 40% base chance of hearing nearby noises, modified by the following:

Obstacle	Modifier
Door	−5%
Wall	−10%
Per 10 feet of distance	−2%

Tactics: In the event of an attack, the ogres' response is haphazard at best. No ogre wishes to appear weak by running for help to his fellows; thus, unless the ogres overhear the sound of battle, they more than likely do not notice anything amiss. Whenever a fight breaks out, the ogres have a 40% base chance of investigating. Modify this by −5% if the sound must go through a door to reach the ogres, by −10% if it must go through a wall, and by −2% for every 10 feet between the ogres and the battle.

To speed things up, make one roll for every five ogres in an area. Assume that the other ogres are simply not paying attention and are too wrapped up in drinking or talking. However, make an individual check for each ogre patrolling **Area 3** and each ogre on watch in **Area 2**, as these fellows are on duty and more alert.

The ogres tend to charge forward in waves when confronted with an attacker. However, if Grimulak is alerted to a battle, the ogres attack with much more cunning. Grimulak's favorite ruse is to split the ogres into two groups and then send them to intercept intruders from two different directions. If a fight erupts in the courtyard, he may send half of the ogres out of the door at **Area 16** to the courtyard and the other half through **Area 18** in hopes of catching the attackers between two groups of warriors.

If confronted with a surprise attack, he orders the ogres to follow him out of the fort, hoping that his enemy thinks the ogres have broken and fled. Soon after, he rallies the ogres and leads them on a counterattack against the fort.

If Grimulak has advance warning of an attack, he uses his *invisibility* to scout the fort and orders his ogres to scatter into small bands and search the fort. If possible, he uses *polymorph self* to change himself into a human child. He tells the characters that he was taken prisoner during the attack of Hansonburg but escaped once he was brought here. He claims he hid in a warehouse at **Area 10** and has managed to avoid the ogres ever since. Once the characters let their guard down or if they run into a group of ogres, Grimulak waits for an opportune moment to unleash his *cone of frost*. If he can get a character alone for a moment, he attempts to use *charm person*. If badly pressed, he uses his ability to fly to escape the fort and flee the region.

The ogres have been quite bored lately, and they eagerly engage the characters in battle. Once 10 or fewer ogres remain, they break and attempt to flee the fort.

ATTACKING OR INFILTRATING THE FORT

Trina and the caravan guards can provide the characters with a rough sketch map of the fort. While they can accompany the characters, Trina points out that a stealthy assault by a few well-armed warriors stands a much better chance against a horde of ogres that managed to conquer the entire fort. If the characters plan on scouting out the fort, returning, and then creating a plan that includes her and the guards, she readily agrees. Under no circumstance does she allow her entire command to enter the fort without thorough reconnaissance.

If Grimulak is taken alive, he tells the characters whatever they want to know to avoid losing his life. He readily agrees to any bargain that results in his going free. He can give the characters information on **Areas 1** and **2** of the first dungeon level (described in **Act III**) and also tells them of how the brain gear first contacted him and how he came to serve it. If asked about the raid on Hansonburg, he denies all knowledge of the attack and blames the bloodthirsty ogres for launching the raid on their own initiative. Of course, the Grimulak helped plan and launch the attack. He's simply smart enough to know that the characters will be much less lenient with him if they think he helped wipe out the village. If the situation seems desperate, he offers the party his *bag of holding* and all of the treasure within: 3,000 gp in coins, a silver coffer inlaid with gems worth 1,000 gp, a gold necklace set with a small red ruby worth 750 gp, and a jade figurine of a small dragon worth 250 gp. Grimulak carries the bag with him at all times.

CHARACTER PLANS

Below are some ideas on common plans and how to handle them:

Divide and Conquer: The characters may use illusions or other tricks to turn the ogres against one another. Careful observation reveals that tempers are running high among the ogres and they seek any chance to come to blows with each other. An ogre has a 4-in-6 chance of attacking another ogre if given a reason to do so, such as a crude insult or a perceived attack. Illusions such as *phantasmal force* can prove very handy for distracting the bored and often inebriated ogres.

Wait Them Out: Morale is quite low among the ogres, and every day 1d4 of them desert the fort. If the characters remain in hiding and wait long enough, they can face a much weaker foe. However, there is a cumulative 10% chance per day that the brain gear creates a new flesh golem and a cumulative 2% chance that it creates a new iron one. Assign these creatures to defend the brain gear at **Area 21** of the dungeon level.

Flesh Golem (if needed): HD 8; HP 40; AC 9[10]; **Atk** 2 fists (2d8); **Move** 8; **Save** 8; **AL** N; **CL/XP** 12/2000; **Special:** +1 or better magic weapons to hit, healed by lightning, slowed by fire and cold, immune to most spells. (*Monstrosities* 219)

Iron Golem (if needed): HD 16; HP 80; AC 3[16]; **Atk** weapon or fist (4d10); **Move** 6; **Save** 3; **AL** N; **CL/XP** 17/3500; **Special:** +2 or better magic weapons to hit, healed by fire, immune to most magic, poison gas (10ft radius cloud, save or die), slowed by lightning. (*Monstrosities* 221)

Poison the Ale or Food: The ogres drink exclusively from the ale kept in **Areas 16** and **17**, plus they gather their food from **Area 10**. Poisoning these supplies is an effective way to spread a venom to all the ogres. In addition, if the food or ale runs out, half the ogres leave the fort each day until none remains, at which point even Grimulak leaves.

Recruit the Captives: The soldiers kept prisoner in **Area 9** are eager to avenge themselves against the ogres though they lack weapons and armor. Note, however that due to starvation and mistreatment, each has only 1d4 hp remaining unless healed.

Aftermath

Once the ogres are driven from the fort, the characters may wish to fortify the place to ensure its security. Trina gladly takes command of this duty. The captives, if rescued by the characters, relate the tale of the fort's fall, confirming Trina's worst fears: Theodocious' experiments have somehow run wild. She insists that the characters head into the dungeons beneath the fort, save Theodocious and anyone else trapped down there, and destroy the wizard's work before it can do any more harm.

If pressed for information on what's down there, Trina knows little. As Theodocious' junior apprentice, she was not allowed to take part in his most secret works. Only Captain Evrik, Theodocious' elder apprentice Bellek, and the master artificer himself were allowed in the dungeons. Trina can draw a map of the first level but knows nothing about the second dungeon level, which Theodocious kept secret even from his apprentices.

The guards eagerly volunteer to help the characters clear the dungeons, but Trina cautions against this, pointing out that the guards would be overmatched against anything down there, and given the cramped spaces, a large group of warriors would only hamper the characters' combat effectiveness. If the characters insist on taking some of the guards down to the dungeon with them, subtract 50 XP from their total for each guard killed in the dungeon, and be sure to divide all XP awards with any guards who survive the dungeon. The penalty is included because, as veteran adventurers, the characters should know that some situations are far too dangerous for novice warriors to face.

ACT III: BENEATH DURGAM'S FOLLY

Once the characters eliminate Grimulak and his ogre minions, they are ready to take on their next challenge. The brain gear is the true threat behind the fall of Durgam's Folly. A wily strategist, it has devised a number of obstacles that those who invade its lair must overcome to meet and defeat it in battle. As noted in the introduction, Orcus has some interest in recovering the brain gear. One of that foul lord's minions is imprisoned within the dungeon beneath the fort and may prove to be a worthwhile, though untrustworthy, ally.

Emphasize the sense of claustrophobia in the dungeons. The corridors are narrow, and the air is hot and moist. The environment here was designed for machines, not living creatures. **Areas 1 through 3** were built along with the rest of the fort by mundane means. Theodocious used *disintegrate* spells along with the help of summoned earth elementals to expand the dungeons. Thus, the first few rooms look hand constructed, while the remaining rooms have a smooth shiny quality to them that suggests a supernatural origin. The doors throughout the complex are high quality and are of superior construction. They can be smashed open with a successful Open Doors check with a –1 penalty. The ceiling throughout the dungeon is 12 feet tall, unless otherwise noted.

The encounter areas described below have little interaction with one another. The brain gear's minions are mostly mindless automatons. While it directs them to some extent, it is often too busy to pay complete attention to their tasks. It fancies itself quite the skilled tactician and is completely confident that the defenses it devised are more than enough to thwart intruders.

If the characters spend a night away from the dungeon, particularly if they want to heal and regain spells, the brain gear is quite active while they are away. For every eight hours they spend out of the dungeon, one out of every 10 clockworks they previously destroyed is repaired and redeployed by the brain gear's minions. Place these monsters as you wish within the dungeon.

1. MEETING ROOM

This room is where the stone golem controlled by the brain gear and Grimulak meet to discuss strategy and the current status of the brain gear's plans. The **4 clockwork warriors** stationed here are under orders to attack any who enter.

Clockwork Warriors (4): HD 3; HP 21, 20, 16x2; AC 2[17]; Atk slam (1d8); Move 9; Save 14; AL N; CL/XP 4/120; Special: self-repair (1hp/round, cannot repair acid, fire or cold damage). (*The Tome of Horrors Complete* 101 or **Appendix B: New Monsters**)

Tactics: The clockworks fight very effectively as a team. Under the brain gear's direction, they swarm toward lightly-armored magic-users, as the brain gear is more than willing to lose a few foot soldiers to destroy a wizard. In addition, the brain gear is keenly aware that a spell such as *fireball* can quickly and permanently destroy his minions.

2. ORGANIC WORKSHOP

The ghastly sight represents the latest experiment by the brain gear: an effort to create clockworks that look human but are actually under the brain gear's control. The poor fellow on the table is barely kept alive by the clockwork organs, though the agony has long since driven him insane. If any characters come close to him, the brain gear seizes control of him and he makes a pitiable attempt to lunge at the offenders. Though the attack is far too weak to threaten the characters, try to catch them off guard and startle them with it.

The brain gear normally takes control of a clockwork and uses it to carry out its experiments and work here.

Perched beneath the table and on the ceiling are **6 clockwork drones**. They attempt to shadow the characters and provide the brain gear with information on their plans and activities.

Clockwork Drones (6): HD 1d6hp; HP 6x2, 5, 4x2, 3; AC 2[17]; Atk slam (1d3); Move 9 (fly 24); Save 18; AL N; CL/XP B/10; Special: none. (*The Tome of Horrors Complete* 99 or **Appendix B: New Monsters**)

3. FAILED EXPERIMENT STORAGE ROOM

The brain gear has spent some time perfecting the art of flesh golem creation, and these unfortunates are all that is left of some of its less successful efforts. A few of the corpses have been infected

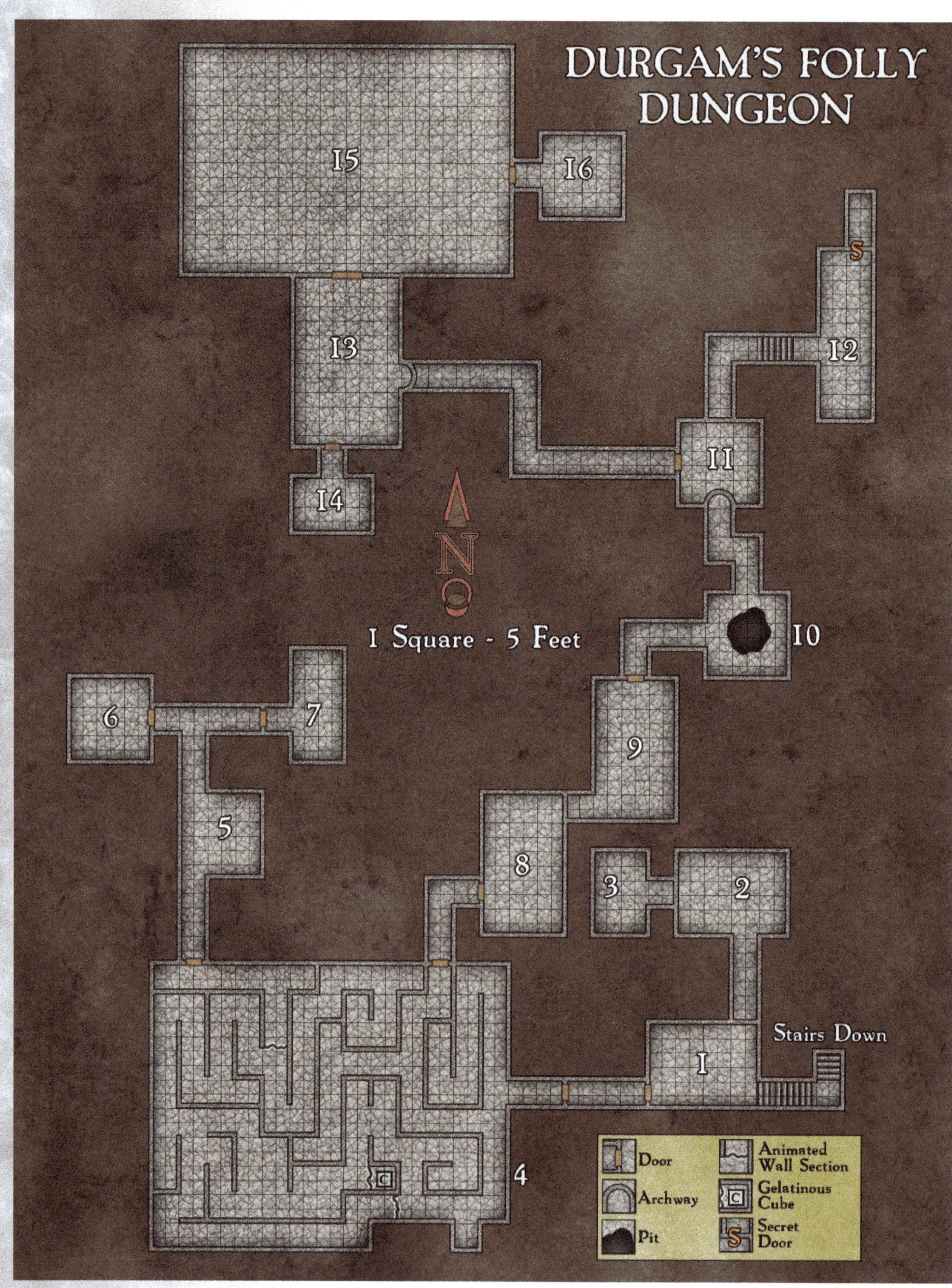

DURGAM'S FOLLY DUNGEON
15
16
S
12
13
14
11
N
1 Square - 5 Feet
10
6
7
9
5
8
3
2
1
Stairs Down
4
C
Door
Archway
Pit
Animated Wall Section
Gelatinous Cube
Secret Door

with the brain gear's latest creation, the clockwork parasites. When the characters file out of the room, the corpses tumble aside as **6 clockwork parasites**, each missing some part of their anatomy other than an arm or leg, shamble after the characters, hoping to catch them from behind. Perhaps the head has been removed or the chest cavity is open and empty. Remember, the clockworks are not undead, so turning attempts do not affect them.

Clockwork Parasites (6): HD 4; HP 22, 19, 18x2, 15, 10; AC 4[15]; **Atk** bite (1d4); **Move** 9; **Save** 13; **AL** N; **CL/XP** 5/240; **Special:** control host (manipulate dead bodies), self-repair (3hp/round after death, cannot heal acid, cold, or fire damage). (***The Tome of Horrors Complete*** 100 or **Appendix B: New Monsters**)

4. THE MAZE

This encounter area is somewhat difficult to run. Be sure to read through the entire description before running it. Note that there is no read-aloud text for this area. Ideally, the characters should have no idea that anything is amiss.

Theodocious struck on the idea that mobile walls could be of tremendous aid in redirecting and confusing invaders. Attackers would move down a corridor that seemed to lead to a passageway ahead only to have the walls shift and lead them elsewhere, while the passage behind them was suddenly blocked. He constructed this maze as a testing ground for this idea and planned on inviting a group of adventurers to test his creation. Now the brain gear controls it and uses it as an important part of its defensive plan. It has added a **gelatinous cube** that it lured here from the lower rooms to a make this trap deadlier.

The maze as it appears on the map shows the starting position of the cube and the three mobile walls that Theodocious built. The mobile walls are built to be indistinguishable from the regular walls, but characters have a 1-in-6 chance to detect something odd about them. Anyone tapping along the walls for secret doors has an easier time detecting them (3-in-6 chance), as they simply sound different when vigorously tapped owing to their construction. The **3 mobile walls** are essentially walls mounted at an angle on wheels. The wall section is mounted on a cart-like contraption that attaches to the back of the wall. When the wall is set to block a corridor, the cart tilts forward, placing the wall while hiding the wheeled cart used to propel it. If discovered, the walls attack and fight to the death, slamming into the characters with great force.

Animated Objects, Mobile Walls (3): HD 4; HP 24, 22x2; AC 4[15]; **Atk** slam (1d8); **Move** 12; **Save** 13; **AL** N; **CL/XP** 4/120; **Special:** none. (***Monstrosities*** 13)

Gelatinous Cube: HD 4; HP 20; AC 8[11]; **Atk** engulf (2d4); **Move** 6; **Save** 13; **AL** N; **CL/XP** 5/240; **Special:** immune to lightning and cold, paralysis (save or paralyzed, 6 turns). (***Monstrosities*** 188)

Tactics: The cube starts in the square marked with a "C." The three mobile walls start as the wall sections marked with an "X." The brain gear coordinates their actions. The walls attempt to lure the characters into the western half of the maze. They then unleash the gelatinous cube and attempt to catch the characters in a dead end.

5. GUARD CHAMBER

The sound of metal scraping against stone echoes down the hallway from the chamber ahead. A great shadowy form moves into view, filling the corridor with its bulk. A crablike metallic automaton lumbers down the corridor toward you, brutal-looking battlefists poised menacingly before its bulk moves to attack. It is only as the thing moves closer that you notice the smaller pair of wood and metal humanoid contraptions that shuffle along before it.

The brain gear ordered a combined unit of clockwork titans and clockwork warriors to hold this chamber against all intruders. They attack anyone who opens the door from **Area 4** south of this chamber.

Tactics: The **2 clockwork titans** and **3 clockwork warriors** assigned to this room work closely together to fight the characters. The warriors form the first rank of fighters, allowing the titans to rain attacks down on the characters while the warriors absorb melee attacks and regenerate. Note, too, that should a warrior fall, it still regenerates and may rise behind a character if they step over a fallen warrior to engage a titan.

Clockwork Titans (2): HD 7; HP 47, 41; AC 0[19]; **Atk** slam (2d8); **Move** 12; **Save** 9; **AL** N; **CL/XP** 8/800; **Special:** none. (***The Tome of Horrors Complete*** 101 or **Appendix B: New Monsters**)

Clockwork Warriors (3): HD 3; HP 22, 18, 16; AC 2[17]; **Atk** slam (1d8); **Move** 9; **Save** 14; **AL** N; **CL/XP** 4/120; **Special:** self-repair (1hp/round, cannot repair acid, fire or cold damage). (***The Tome of Horrors Complete*** 101 or **Appendix B: New Monsters**)

6. HOLDING CELL

The air before you is thick with a vaguely blue haze. You can feel great tension in the air, as if a thunderstorm were about to erupt in this room, battering it with lightning and drenching it with a torrential downpour. Through the mist, you can see a humanoid figure struggling fiercely, as if it is attempting to sunder a set of chains that hold it in place.

The creature trapped here is **Gorrush Kar**, a demon-wolf of Braazz and a minor lieutenant in the dread demon's infernal legion. He is the last surviving member of the team sent by Orcus to investigate the brain gear. He appears as a six-foot-six-inch-tall human with crimson skin, short pointed horns, and eight-inch-long red fingernails. His face is vaguely wolf-like. He wears only a black loincloth and is unarmed. The clockworks chained him here, and the brain gear activated a series of powerful runes Theodocious had inscribed here that prevent fiends from using their natural magical abilities. The chains that bind Gorrush are made of iron. They can be broken with a successful Open Doors check.

Gorrush begs for his freedom in a low, rasping voice. While diabolical to the core, he knows when he is outclassed and is willing to work with the characters to gain his vengeance against the brain gear. The fiend tries to convince the characters to allow him to accompany them, telling them that he has special knowledge of the brain gear's weakness. In truth, he knows only that the brain gear is merely a magical intelligence encased in a copper box, rather than a clockwork or stone golem. (The brain gear commonly possesses the form of an unfinished stone golem. See **Areas 14**, **15**, and **16** for more details.) Gorrush claims any number of things to sway the characters, including but not limited to claims that he has converted away from the cause of evil or that he is merely a victim of the brain gear, much like the characters.

If Gorrush accompanies the characters, he carefully watches them in battle. If they appear competent, he works with them to find the brain gear. He attempts to appear useful but keeps back from the fighting, unwilling to risk himself for the characters. Once in combat against it, he waits for the characters to engage the brain gear's stone golem before rushing forward to grab the brain gear's case and *gate* to Orcus's realm. If the characters destroy the brain gear, he attempts to flee the dungeon if the characters have turned against him. Otherwise, he waits for an opportune moment to steal as much of the characters' wealth as possible before slipping away into the wilderness.

Gorrush Kar, Demon-Wolf of Braazz: HD 5; HP 33; AC 1[18]; Atk bite (1d10); **Move** 15; **Save** 12; **AL** C; **CL/XP** 8/800; **Special:** +1 or better magic weapons to hit, blink (1/day, *teleport* 30ft), *charm person* (gaze, as spell, save resists), *gate* (1 time, returns to Orcus), *invisibility* (3/day), shapechange (humanoid or wolf-like forms). (***Monstrosities*** 114)

7. STONE CHAMBER

This room is stacked high with lumber, iron ingots, sacks of nails, rope, and other supplies. A suit of chainmail hangs from a hook near the door, and a bronze battleaxe whose head has been modified to look like a leering demon's head, its elephantine ears serving as the double-bladed axe's cutting edges, leans against the wall.

The brain gear uses this room as a place to store raw materials necessary to construct new clockworks. The battleaxe belongs to Gorrush, and he claims it as his own if the fiend is with the party. If the characters make a thorough search of this room, they find a locked wooden chest containing a suit of *+1 chainmail* and three potions: *clairvoyance*, *extra healing*, and *heroism*. The chest can be opened with thieves' tools. Theodocious kept these valuables here, and with the brain gear's revolt they have been forgotten.

8. WORKROOM

The floor of this room is covered with sawdust, cast-off pieces of lumber ,and bent nails. Two long workbenches stand on the eastern and western walls. A humanoid-shaped wood and metal contraption draped with torn, red robes stands before the eastern bench, carefully carving a piece of wood.

The clockwork creature was once Theodocious' apprentice **Bellek**. The brain gear removed his brain and installed it within a clockwork. Observant characters can note that human blood drips down the clockwork's head and spreads across its frame and robes. Now a half-mad thrall of the clockwork, the apprentice lashes out at intruders with his remaining magic spells. As the apprentice attacks, **3 clockwork warriors** shuffle through the door leading to **Area 9** and move to attack the characters and defend the apprentice.

Bellek, Clockwork Creature (MU5): HD 5; HP 34; AC 2[17]; **Atk** dagger (1d4); **Move** 9; **Save** 13; **AL** N; **CL/XP** 5/240; **Special:** spells (4/2/1). (see **Appendix B: New Monsters**)
Spells: 1st—*charm person, magic missile* (x2), *sleep*; 2nd—*phantasmal force, strength*; 3rd—*lightning bolt*.

Clockwork Warriors (3): HD 3; HP 20, 17, 13; AC 2[17]; **Atk** slam (1d8); **Move** 9; **Save** 14; **AL** N; **CL/XP** 4/120; **Special:** self-repair (1hp/round, cannot repair acid, fire or cold damage). (***The Tome of Horrors Complete*** 101 or **Appendix B: New Monsters**)

9. CHAMBER OF THEODOCIOUS THE FORGER

In this room, a clockwork contraption wearing gray robes and outfitted with what looks like a beard made of white cotton stands over a large, low-lying table. Lying on the table is the half-completed form of a clockwork warrior. The robe-clad clockwork looks up at you, seeming to almost sag visibly as it peers at you. From out of the shadows to the north strides a tall, sleek-looking construct. Its polished steel frame reflects your own image back at you.

The robe-clad clockwork is **Theodocious**, or what remains of him. Forced into servitude much like his apprentice Bellek, the archmage now seeks only death to release him from servitude. While incapable of speech, Theodocious attempts to make his wishes known as clearly as possible to the characters. Unfortunately for the part, his **2 clockwork titans** do not let Theodocious go down without a fight. They step in front of the clockwork magic-user every chance they gets to either absorb any damage with their metal bodies.

If given a quill and parchment, Theodocious writes a note begging the characters to destroy him. He offers to point them in the direction of a magical item that may help them destroy the brain gear. Hidden beneath Theodocious' robes are two *bolts of shattering* (see **Appendix A: New Magic Item**) and a parchment that describes the brain gear's true nature and reveals the stone golem as little more than an empty vessel for its commands (see **Areas 14, 15,** and **16** for details). Theodocious penned the note in hopes that someone powerful enough to defeat his shield guardian, and thus mighty enough to take on the brain gear, would someday come along to end his misery. Half-mad with pain and torn by grief at what his creation has become, the archmage seeks the peaceful oblivion of death. He considers the information he has on the brain gear a fair trade for his final destruction and refuses to divulge his items or gear to the characters before they destroy him. He mentions information to pique their interest but does not reveal that he carries the items on his person, telling the characters instead that he can pass it along to them when the shield guardian is destroyed.

Theodocious, Clockwork Creature (MU12): HD 12; HP 87; AC 2[17]; **Atk** dagger (1d4); **Move** 9; **Save** 13; **AL** N; **CL/XP** 12/2000; **Special:** none. (see **Appendix B: New Monsters**)
Note: Theodocious wants to be destroyed and doesn't fight back. He has no spells prepared.

Clockwork Titans (2): HD 7; HP 51, 50; AC 0[19]; **Atk** slam (2d8); **Move** 12; **Save** 9; **AL** N; **CL/XP** 8/800; **Special:** none. (***The Tome of Horrors Complete*** 101 or **Appendix B: New Monsters**)

Note: The clockwork titans have a 4-in-6 chance of stepping in front of any spell or attack directed at Theodocious to absorb any damage directed at the magic-user.

Tactics: The titans relentlessly attack anyone who threatens Theodocious, ceasing their assaults only when the attackers leave the room. They continue to protect Theodosius' dead body. The things refuse to let Theodocious out of their sight.

Don't award the characters any XP for destroying Theodocious, as the wizard makes no attempt to resist their attacks and has no spells prepared.

10. ACCESS PIT

> This room looks as if it served as the dumping ground for a mad inventor. Wooden beams, broken weapons, battered and cracked suits of armor, and other half-wrecked pieces of equipment litter the floor here, literally knee deep across the room. However, a five-foot-wide area has been cleared out directly in the center of the room. From your vantage point, it looks as if there is a hole in the floor there. To the right, a passageway opens up in the center of the north wall.

The garbage throughout the room is two feet deep. Theodocious used this room to store the results of failed experiments. While attempting to expand this room so it could hold more garbage, he opened a hole in the north wall with a *disintegrate* spell and gained access to the forgotten temple deep below Durgam's Folly. The pit in the center of the room was added to increase the capacity of this room. It is 20 feet deep and filled with five feet of garbage.

Lurking within the garbage are **3 clockwork swarms**, tiny colonies of clockworks that can rapidly create jury-rigged clockwork machines. The swarms use the garbage to form rigs capable of battling the characters. The clockworks then wait until the characters are close to the pit, then they surge from the garbage, seeking to knock characters down into the pit before scrambling after them for the kill. The swarms are nearly impossible to see in the garbage, although the characters can note a few tiny clockworks scurrying about.

Clockwork Swarms (3): HD 4; HP 30, 28, 27; AC 2[17]; **Atk** swarm (1d6); **Move** 15; **Save** 13; **AL** N; **CL/XP** 7/600; **Special:** distraction (save after successful swarm attack or stunned for 1 round), resists slashing and piercing weapons (50%), self-repair (3hp/round, cannot repair acid, cold, or fire damage). (*The Tome of Horrors Complete* 101 or **Appendix B: New Monsters**)

11. ACCESS ROOM

> Suddenly, the stonework of the passage gives way to a deep, black rock. Your light source gains a sickly greenish tinge to it as you enter this 15-foot-by-15-foot room. Bronze doors stand in the middle of the north and west walls. Each of the doors is intricately detailed with a leering demonic visage.

This is the first chamber of the old temple. The western door opens easily, but the northern door is locked shut. The lock is rather difficult to pick (–15% Open Locks). The doors here are quite stout, as they are made of bronze rather than wood. They can be broken down with a

This area of the dungeon was once a hidden temple devoted to demonic powers, including Orcus. Many years ago, a great champion of good destroyed the temple's residents and used powerful magic to seal it beneath a mound of earth. Durgam's Folly was built upon the resulting hill, and Theodocious' delving reopened the temple. Its strong aura of evil magic helped twist the brain gear and turn it to evil. Paladins and good clerics can almost feel the evil atmosphere as a tangible presence; *detect evil* reveals the entire place as evil. The stonework here is much older than the previous rooms and somewhat dustier, as far fewer creatures or clockworks have walked these hallways. The brain gear dwells here for defensive purposes and because it finds the evil-tainted atmosphere somewhat soothing.

successful Open Doors check with a –2 penalty. The north door is kept locked to keep a rogue, berserk flesh golem safely contained in **Area 12**. The door is somewhat pushed out of its frame, as if something from the opposite side tried to batter it down. For every five minutes the characters spend in this room, there is a cumulative 25% chance the golem begins beating on the north door from the opposite side. The golem has a 1-in-6 chance of breaking through the door.

12. CHAMBER OF THE FLESH GOLEM

This long, narrow room is hewn from the same black stone as the rest of this area of the dungeon. A tall, stooped figure in blood-stained blue robes staggers about the room. Suddenly, it seems to notice you and turns in your direction. As it faces you, you can see that the figure is bleeding from scores of wounds in its chest and face, all of which have been hastily stitched shut. The figure lets out an enraged cry as it charges toward you, fists raised in fury.

This **flesh golem** was one of the brain gear's first experiments. After it went rogue, the brain gear managed to herd it into this room and lock it here with the use of its stone golem. It hopes someday to determine the cause of the flesh golem's berserk rage and repair it. Until then, the creature resides here.

The secret door in this room's north wall hides a small cache of gold and treasure left over from the temple's days as a powerful center of evil power. It contains 2,000 gp stashed in a copper chest worth 300 gp, a *+1 warhammer*, and a scroll of three spells: *cure light wounds*, *raise dead*, and *hold person*.

Flesh Golem: HD 8; HP 40; AC 9[10]; Atk 2 fists (2d8); **Move** 8; **Save** 8; **AL** N; **CL/XP** 12/2000; **Special:** +1 or better magic weapons to hit, healed by lightning, slowed by fire and cold, immune to most spells. (*Monstrosities* 219)

13. TEMPLE FOYER

The black rock in this chamber is streaked with misty red lines. Your light casts a reddish glow here, and the air is damp and oppressive. To the north is a pair of bronze double doors, while on the south wall stands a tall and narrow bronze door. As you scan the room, you have the strange feeling that the red streaks on the wall throb and undulate just at the edge of your field of vision, but when you turn to look at them, you see nothing amiss.

This room once served as a gathering place for the temple's dark disciples. Now it is the brain gear's penultimate line of defense. When the characters attempt to open the northern doors, the **flesh golem** from **Area 14** rushes out to attack them, bellowing in rage. At the same time, the **stone golem** in **Area 15** moves forward under the brain gear's control, ready to attack. The brain gear plans to trap the characters in **Area 13** and destroy them before they have any chance to threaten its physical case in **Area 16**. The flesh golem peers into **Area 13** through the keyhole set in the door to **Area 14**. Anyone searching the southern door for traps notices the golem's blank eye staring back through the keyhole. The golem has been specifically ordered not to attack until the double doors or the south door is opened. Thus, it takes no actions if the characters discover it before opening the door, unless they target it with attacks or spells through the keyhole.

If the characters try the south door first, the flesh golem still rushes out to attack. However, the stone golem waits a full five rounds before committing itself to battle, as the brain gear hopes that the characters will become so preoccupied with the flesh golem that they will leave themselves vulnerable to an attack from the north.

The stone golem is a construct specifically created by Theodocious for the brain gear. The brain gear can control the stone golem, much like a clockwork, so long as it is within two miles of the brain gear. In addition, the brain gear can speak while in control of the stone golem, using the construct not only as a powerful battle machine but also as its mobile voice. The brain gear uses the stone golem to meet and communicate with Grimulak, and it plans to continue to use it as a "spokesgolem" in the future. Feel free to allow the brain gear to gloat over the characters or otherwise reinforce the illusion that the stone golem is actually the brain gear. The brain gear looks down upon organic life as pitiable and weak and takes every opportunity to demonstrate its superiority through both words and actions. It taunts the characters and comments on how useful their bodies may be in constructing more flesh golems.

The stone golem's primary aim is to keep the characters from moving into **Area 15** and from there into **Area 16**, where the brain gear sits. The golems are more than likely a match for the characters, and if the party goes toe to toe with them they may very well be destroyed. If the characters aided Theodocious, they should have at least some idea that fighting the stone golem is fruitless. In addition, if Gorrush Kar is with the party, he immediately rushes past the stone golem and heads to **Area 16** seeking to claim the brain gear for his master. Most importantly, if the stone golem moves more than two miles from the brain gear (which happens if, for example, the brain gear was suddenly *gated* to the Abyss), the golem instantly collapses into pieces. This also occurs if the characters destroy the brain gear. Note that the flesh golem remains intact, as it is not a clockwork, and it continues to attack the characters.

Flesh Golem: HD 8; HP 40; AC 9[10]; Atk 2 fists (2d8); **Move** 8; **Save** 8; **AL** N; **CL/XP** 12/2000; **Special:** +1 or better magic weapons to hit, healed by lightning, slowed by fire and cold, immune to most spells. (*Monstrosities* 219)

Stone Golem: **HD** 12; **HP** 60; **AC** 5[14]; **Atk** fist (3d8);
Move 6; **Save** 3; **CL/XP** 16/3200; **Special:** +2 or better
magic weapon to hit, immune to most magic (slowed by fire,
damaged by rock to mud). (**Monstrosities** 222)

14. Temple Closet

This small room is bare of all furnishings and
decorations. A plain wooden stool sits before the doorway,
looking somewhat out of place in this dark dungeon.

This room is completely bare. The flesh golem keeps its watch
while squatting on the stool, waiting for intruders to enter **Area 13** and
spur it into action. If the characters somehow enter this room without
opening the door, the golem ignores them and continues to keep a
careful eye on **Area 13**. Of course, if it is subsequently attacked it
defends itself.

15. Temple of Darkness

The **stone golem** stands here near the double doors, waiting to
attack any intruders. This temple was long since thrown down by the
forces of good, yet the corrupting influence of the dark powers can
never be truly cleansed from this place.

This large chamber's vaulted ceiling rises above you,
giving you an immediate sense of open space while at the
same time almost suffocating you with an intense aura
of dread and foreboding. Rows of stone pews stand in
neat rows all facing a black, basalt altar at the eastern
end of this room. A large stone goat's head is carved into
the eastern wall. Just beneath the idol is a plain-looking
bronze door.

The stone golem goes to great efforts to prevent any characters from
reaching the door to the east. However, if the characters attempt to
enter the door, the brain gear enters a bit of panic. It madly rushes the
stone golem about, chasing down anyone who enters the room. Given
the stone golem's slow movement and inability to run, most characters
should be able to outrun it and buy a single character enough time
to enter **Area 16**. The golem immediately charges after anyone who
enters that room, ignoring all other threats.

16. Inner Sanctum

A plain wooden table sits in the center of this small, square chamber.
Set upon the table is a cube of copper surrounded by a pale blue nimbus
of magical power. Beneath the table stands a plain wooden chest.

The copper cube sitting on the table contains the magical essence
of the **brain gear**. Smashing the cube disrupts the brain gear and
destroys it forever.

Clockwork Brain Gear: **HD** 5; **HP** 35; **AC** 2[17]; **Atk** none;
Move 0 (immobile); **Save** 12; **CL/XP** 5/240; **Special:** control
clockworks, dream (send psychic messages). (**The Tome of
Horrors Complete** 99)

Treasure: The unlocked wooden chest contains the brain gear's
current treasury. The chest holds 3,000 gp in coins; a set of emerald
earrings worth 300 gp; a 16-inch-tall golden idol of a goat-headed
humanoid worth 1,200 gp; a black velvet bag containing eight
small diamonds, each worth 150 gp; a single large ruby worth
4,000 gp; a jeweled dagger worth 300 gp; and six golden ingots
worth 500 gp each.

Concluding the Adventure

Once the brain gear is destroyed or taken to the Abyss, the clockworks
collapse into little more than spare parts. While the animated walls in
Area 4 and the flesh golems still operate, the rest of the brain gear's
minions fall to pieces. If the characters sent for reinforcements to
retake the fort, they soon appear, and while the ruling house attempts
to keep the facts surrounding this incident quiet, the characters are
handsomely rewarded for their efforts, each receiving 10,000 gp in
either coins or goods.

While this adventure is over, the story of the brain gear is by no
means complete. Here are some ideas for continuing campaign play
involving characters introduced in this module:

• If Gorrush Kar escaped with the brain gear, Orcus and his minions
waste little time in decoding the secret of its manufacture. Orcus orders
the construction of a great workshop dedicated to forging new brain
gears and clockwork minions. The demon lord plans to use them as
part of his infernal legions and earmarks several of the brain gears to
establish beachheads in the characters' homeland. Soon, clockworks
are reported raiding communities in the Borderlands Provinces.

• If Gorrush Kar did not seize the brain gear but survived the
adventure, he may swear vengeance against the characters and work
to destroy them. His mission for Orcus was unfulfilled; the fiend has
little choice but to remain in the Prime Material Plane. He cannot
return to the Abyss without facing Orcus' wrath. The wily fiend allies
with whatever evil patron he can find and works tirelessly to ensure
that he crosses paths with the characters in the future. Perhaps he plots
to kidnap the characters' family members or other loved ones.

• Perhaps there are even more undiscovered galleries hidden
beneath Durgam's Folly. Concerned for the fort's future security, the
new commander asks the characters to explore the depths. An ancient
lich lives deep beneath the fort, served by a variety of undead. In
this realm of the dead, the lich is king and his court is composed of
mummies, ghouls, and worse.

Appendix A: New Magic Item

This appendix describes a new magic item found in this module.

Unusual Missile Weapon

Bolt of Shattering

These magical crossbow bolts look like regular missiles forged wholly from steel. If a target hit by a *bolt of shattering* is a construct, the target suffers 4d8 points of explosive damage in addition to the damage the bolt normally does. After dealing this bonus damage, the *bolt of shattering* become a normal non-magical crossbow bolt.

Appendix B: New Monsters

This appendix describes the new creatures found in this adventure.

Clockwork Brain Gear

Hit Dice: 5
Armor Class: 2[17]
Attack: None
Saving Throw: 12
Special: Control clockworks, dream
Move: 0
Alignment: Neutrality
Challenge Level/XP: 3/60

The brain gear began as little more than a disparate collection of gears, chains, counterweights, and levers. Theodocious sought to replicate and improve on the process used to grant golems their limited independence. Consulting an ancient text of golem lore, Theodocious constructed the thinking element of a golem, dubbed the brain gear, with two important changes. First, he built the brain gear on a much larger than normal scale, allowing him to create a more complex brain than regular magical routines could allow for. Second, rather than create a brain solely from the essence of magic, Theodocious manufactured large parts of it with mechanical constructs to create a more durable, easier to produce, and cheaper design. Unfortunately, Theodocious failed to account for an important variable. A golem's mental essence is normally created from magic because the process involved is as foolproof as possible. Given how unstable golems can be, particularly flesh and clay ones, adding further nonmagical variables to the mix only increased the instability and unreliability of the brain gear. Theodocious hoped to combat this effect by using magical items and historical artifacts from honorable heroes and brilliant generals. If the brain gear's physical essence were composed of items with honorable legacies, Theodocious reasoned, then the brain gear's mental essence would follow suit.

Unfortunately for Theodocious and the garrison, the brain gear developed a malevolent intelligence and quickly threw off the controls Theodocious placed upon it. However, the gear was far too wily to lash out at its creator. For the first week of its life, it spent many hours pondering the riddle of its existence. The items used to construct the gear had a radically different effect on its development than Theodocious expected. The brain gear absorbed the ambient memories and deeds associated with the items. From them, it grew to love conflict, war, and tactics, as Theodocious had hoped. However, rather than forming an affection and kinship with humanity, under the influence of the dark forces Theodocious accidentally unleashed, it learned that the vast majority of humans are weak, fractious, and self-centered. The brain gear decided that it had no desire to serve such masters. True, the occasional hero broke the typical human mold, but the brain gear reasoned that it had but a miniscule chance of ever falling under the leadership of a true hero. Instead, it decided to forge its own fate. In secret, it built its army of servitors. Using them as its eyes and ears and drawing upon the tactical and strategic lessons it learned from its inherited memories, the brain gear struck without warning, overwhelming the garrison and killing or capturing every last living thing in a matter of minutes.

The brain gear is now primarily concerned with improving its own capabilities in order to launch its own campaign of conquest across the land. The brain gear is smart enough to know that when weeks pass without word from the fort, someone will arrive to investigate. To give itself the best chance at victory in its unavoidable conflicts with outsiders, the brain gear has retreated into the dungeon level of the fort. There it has further modified itself, expanding to take up several rooms and building more guardians to man the fort. The upper level of the fort has been given over to defensive constructs.

Statistics: The brain gear is a large thinking machine, not unlike the vintage, room-sized computers of the 1950s. Destroying a brain gear is rather simple in theory. Smashing the gear's primary casing — a copper box two feet long and a foot tall that contains the magical essence of the gear's personality — is enough to disperse the gear and bring its minions to a grinding halt.

By itself, the brain gear is little threat to adventurers. It is immobile, it has no attacks, and is largely incapable of harming its opponents. The brain gear relies on its clockworks to defend it from invaders and further its plans. However, since clockworks farther than two miles away from the brain gear fall out of its control, the gear must ally with organic beings to influence the world around it.

The brain gear serves as a mastermind that hides behind others when opposing the characters.

Abilities: The brain gear is gifted with a few special abilities. First, it can take control of other constructs designed by Theodocious, as it was designed to interact with them and command them much like a general. Any clockwork construct that comes within two miles of a brain gear immediately falls under that gear's control. If more than one gear is in the area, randomly determine which one claims the wayward clockwork. When a clockwork moves more than two miles away from a brain gear, it continues to perform the last order it was given, but there is a 25% chance per hour that it ceases to function and collapses into a pile of junk. If a brain gear later moves within two miles of the destroyed clockwork, the clockwork can reactivate if it has the self-repair ability. Otherwise, it is permanently destroyed.

The brain gear can take direct control of any clockwork within two miles of its position. It can use this ability to instantaneously jump from clockwork to clockwork, keeping tabs on all of its thralls and seeing the world through their senses. The brain gear can switch control from one clockwork to another once per round as a free action. The brain gear uses this ability to give commands to its clockworks, allowing the usually mindless creatures to fight with highly-coordinated tactics. Each clockwork is capable of receiving roughly 100 words worth of orders. Anything beyond that is too complicated for the clockwork to handle.

The brain gear also has limited ability to send psychic messages to organic creatures. Once per week, it can send a psychic message in a dream. The brain gear can contact multiple creatures.

Clockwork Brain Gear: HD 5; HP 35; AC 2[17]; **Atk** none; Move 0 (immobile); **Save** 12; CL/XP 5/240; **Special:** control clockworks, dream (send psychic messages). (*The Tome of Horrors Complete* 99)

Clockwork Creature

Hit Dice: 2
Armor Class: 2[17]
Attack: Slam (1d4)
Saving Throw: 16
Special: None
Move: 9
Alignment: Neutrality
Challenge Level/XP: 2/30

Clockwork creatures are living things that have been converted into mechanical monstrosities by the brain gear. They are gruesome in appearance, as the brain gear installs its victim's brain and a few vital organs, such as the heart, into a mechanical shell. The resulting creation looks like a ghoulish clockwork creature. Its outer hull has the appearance of a humanoid iron and wood contraption, but the red blood that oozes from its joints and the pained cries for a merciful death that emanate from the clockwork betray its organic origin.

Clockwork creatures are an experimental attempt by the brain gear to improve on existing clockwork designs. The brain gear hopes to create the ultimate slave, a servant with the intelligence and flexibility of an organic creature but the unthinking obedience and slavish devotion of a clockwork.

Some clockwork creatures retain the spellcasting abilities of their host brain.

Clockwork Drone

Hit Dice: 1d6
Armor Class: 2[17]
Attack: Slam (1d3)
Saving Throw: 18
Special: None
Move: 9/24 (flying)
Alignment: Neutrality
Challenge Level/XP: B/10

The clockwork drone is a human eyeball encased within a flat, metal disk. Imbued with magic that allows it to fly, the drone's approach is typically marked by the low buzz of its tiny gears and pistons, which work furiously to maintain the magical field that allows it to fly. These clockworks are designed to act as observers. When the drone finds an advantageous position from which to maintain its watch, it uses a small, metallic claw on its underside to attach itself to a surface.

Drones usually avoid combat at all costs. When pressed into fighting, they prefer to aid their fellow clockworks by distracting their enemies.

Clockwork Drone: HD 1d6hp; AC 2[17]; **Atk** slam (1d3); Move 9 (fly 24); Save 18; AL N; CL/XP B/10; **Special:** none. (*The Tome of Horrors Complete* 99)

Clockwork Overseer

Hit Dice: 2
Armor Class: 2[17]
Attack: Slam (1d6)
Saving Throw: 16
Special: None
Move: 15
Alignment: Neutrality
Challenge Level/XP: 2/30

The overseers are a recent invention of the brain gear. Theodocious never meant for the brain gear to control clockworks beyond a limited area. The first order of business for the ambitious, power-hungry brain gear was to create a new type of clockwork that could overcome this limitation. The overseer clockwork resulted from the brain gear's research. The overseer can journey up to 10 miles away from the brain gear while maintaining contact with it. In addition, the overseer acts as a sort of field commander for the brain gear, controlling clockworks beyond the brain gear's reach. The brain gear plans to improve the overseers, hoping to extend the range and allow for the creation of fully functional armies that can terrorize civilized lands.

The overseer looks like a three-foot-tall wooden doll with long, slender limbs. It moves with uncanny grace and a speed and fluidity that belies its mechanical origin.

The overseer avoids direct combat at all costs. The brain gear expended considerable time and resources designing it, and it is thus under orders to avoid fighting. Unless backed into a corner with no escape route, the overseer attempts to flee.

Independent Clockwork. As described above, the overseer can move beyond the brain gear's normal area of influence while maintaining contact with it. Normally, the brain gear can control only clockworks that are within two miles of its position. The brain gear can control an overseer that stays within 10 miles of its position. In addition, the overseer can act as a field commander for up to 20 hit dice worth of clockworks that are within 100 feet of its position. These clockworks are considered to be in contact with it.

Clockwork Overseer: HD 2; AC 2[17]; **Atk** slam (1d6); **Move** 15; **Save** 16; AL N; CL/XP 2/30; **Special:** none. (*The Tome of Horrors Complete* 99)

Clockwork Parasites (The Possessed)

Hit Dice: 4
Armor Class: 4[15]
Attack: Bite (1d4)
Saving Throw: 13
Special: Control host, self-repair
Move: 9
Alignment: Neutrality
Challenge Level/XP: 5/240

Clockwork parasites are fist-sized constructs that resemble mechanical beetles. They burrow into the skulls of the recently dead and reanimate the body using electrical impulses to control and direct the corpse. The animated corpses look and fight like zombies, though they cannot be turned or controlled. A host that is brought to 0 or fewer hit points is destroyed, but the clockwork parasite can repair the host using its self-repair ability. A clockwork parasite regains 3 hit points per round, but this repair begins only after the host is killed. Damage dealt from acid, cold, or fire effects cannot be self-repaired.

Clockwork Parasite: HD 4; AC 4[15]; Atk bite (1d4); Move 9; Save 13; AL N; CL/XP 5/240; Special: control host (manipulate dead bodies), self-repair (3hp/round after death, cannot heal acid, cold, or fire damage). (*The Tome of Horrors Complete* 100)

Clockwork Scout

Hit Dice: 1
Armor Class: 2[17]
Attack: Slam (1d4)
Saving Throw: 17
Special: None
Move: 15
Alignment: Neutrality
Challenge Level/XP: 1/15

Clockwork scouts are designed to serve as the mobile eyes and ears of the clockwork colony. While still restricted by the two-mile radius they must remain within to keep contact with the brain gear, scouts serve an important role as reconnaissance, patrol, and pursuit troops.

Scouts are constructed to resemble animals commonly found in the area that the brain gear operates within. This camouflage helps them move about unnoticed and gives them the opportunity to strike from ambush. Characters have only a 1-in-6 chance to notice the deception (2-in-6 for demi-humans, and 3-in-6 for druids and rangers).

Clockwork scouts prefer to attack from ambush. Often, they climb trees and leap down upon opponents. If they come across an enemy, the brain gear may direct them to sneak into the camp and steal equipment or carry off water, food, and other necessities. Usually, the brain gear prefers to hold scouts back from combat. Only if the scouts have a chance to strike from a devastating ambush does the brain gear order them into battle.

Clockwork Scout: HD 1; AC 2[17]; Atk slam (1d4); Move 15; Save 17; AL N; CL/XP 1/15; Special: camouflage (1-in-2 chance to notice; 2-in-6 for elves, dwarves and halflings; 3-in-6 for rangers and druids). (*The Tome of Horrors Complete* 100)

Clockwork Swarm

Hit Dice: 4
Armor Class: 2[17]
Attack: Swarm (1d6)
Saving Throw: 13
Special: Distraction, minimum damage from slashing and piercing weapons, self-repair
Move: 15
Alignment: Neutrality
Challenge Level/XP: 7/600

Clockwork swarms are a collection of tiny, insect-looking clockworks that work together as a single creature. An individual member of the swarm poses little threat. But when acting in concert, the swarm poses a deadly threat to adventurers. Much like the clockwork warrior, the clockwork swarm forms a fighting frame from random pieces of trash, debris, and other cast-offs. The swarm, however, is much more capable of adapting to new situations and surviving combat. Unless the individual components of the swarm are destroyed, it simply reforms and continues to attack. Area of effect attacks such as burning oil, *fireball*, or *lightning bolt* are the most effective means of destroying the swarm.

A clockwork swarm typically appears as a ramshackle collection of spare parts and garbage draped in a thick, web-like substance and arranged in a vaguely humanoid form. Living creatures engulfed by the clockwork swarm must succeed on a saving throw or be unable to act during that round.

The swarm prefers to lie in wait and strike from ambush, collecting innocuous-looking piles of debris that adventurers overlook as harmless but that the swarm is capable of quickly forming into a combat-worthy frame.

A clockwork swarm regains 3 hit points per round. Damage dealt from acid, cold, or fire effects cannot be self-repaired. If a clockwork swarm takes damage from an area attack, it is unable to repair itself for 1d6 rounds following the attack.

Clockwork Swarm: HD 4; AC 2[17]; Atk swarm (1d6); Move 15; Save 13; AL N; CL/XP 7/600; Special: distraction (save after successful swarm attack or stunned for 1 round), resists slashing and piercing weapons (50%), self-repair (3hp/round, cannot repair acid, cold, or fire damage). (*The Tome of Horrors Complete* 101)

Clockwork Titan

Hit Dice: 7
Armor Class: 0[19]
Attack: Slam (2d8)
Saving Throw: 9
Special: None
Move: 12
Alignment: Neutrality
Challenge Level/XP: 8/800

The clockwork titan appears as a huge, crablike, mechanical monstrosity. The titan has a saucer-shaped main hull with four spindly legs that sprout from its underbelly and allow the titan to move with surprising speed and agility.

Two iron-shod fists are mounted on the front of the titan's hull, giving it excellent reach in combat. In battle, the clockwork titan relies on its reach to keep opponents back. Quite often, the brain gear attempts to deploy its titans to rain blows upon enemies without fear of any counterattack.

Clockwork Titan: HD 7; AC 0[19]; **Atk** slam (2d8); **Move** 12; **Save** 9; **AL** N; **CL/XP** 8/800; **Special:** none. (*The Tome of Horrors Complete* 101)

CLOCKWORK WARRIOR

Hit Dice: 3
Armor Class: 2[17]
Attack: Slam (1d8)
Saving Throw: 14
Special: Self-repair
Move: 9
Alignment: Neutrality
Challenge Level/XP: 4/120

Clockwork warriors are constructed from a wide range of materials but take the same general form of a six-foot-tall humanoid with oversized hands and a stiff, shambling gait. In battle, clockwork warriors rely on relentless wave attacks to overwhelm their foes. They are far too slow to engage faster units and usually serve as the primarily defensive troops for a clockwork colony. Clockwork warriors are usually formed of cast-off equipment and detritus scavenged from battlefields. They all feature a "nervous system" of thin steel wires that control the clockwork's individual pieces. Tiny clockworks that look much like metallic cockroaches infest the warrior, working to repair 1 hit point of damage per round and are capable of rebuilding a destroyed clockwork given enough time. Acid, cold, and fire attacks destroy these maintenance clockworks and prevent the warrior from regenerating damage. Unlike clockwork swarms, the clockworks that repair the warrior lack the intelligence and sophistication to tackle any other task.

Clockwork Warrior: HD 3; AC 2[17]; **Atk** slam (1d8); **Move** 9; **Save** 14; **AL** N; **CL/XP** 4/120; **Special:** self-repair (1hp/ round, cannot repair acid, fire or cold damage). (*The Tome of Horrors Complete* 101)

Appendix C: Option Pack

by Björn Strohecker

Introduction

The Siege of Durgam's Folly includes a wilderness area to cross, a fort to free from an enemy's hands (or to defend from them), and a tricky dungeon full of bizarre and surprising encounters to explore. Maybe you want to challenge your players even more by adding a couple of options intended to raise the overall difficulty of the adventure? Consider carefully if your players — and foremost their characters — are experienced enough to handle these extra challenges. Most of the material herein should make them sweat more than just a little …

Option 1: Ogres on Guard!

With this option, the ogres are expecting retribution for the destruction of Hansonburg and the brutal murder of its citizens, contrary to the behavior described in the original adventure.

The main gate is not open, and the ogres are on watch. On watch atop each tower are **3** or **4 ogres**, and two units of **2 ogres** each regularly patrol in the main courtyard (**Area 3**). The gatehouse (**Area 2**) is guarded by **2 ogres**. Additionally, **2 ogres** are guarding the entrance to the tower (**Area 9**) where the prisoners are kept. If the party has any means to spy on the fort before entering it, these two guards may provide the clue the characters need to locate the prisoners. Any ogre who detects an enemy within Durgam's Folly or its perimeter immediately cries out an alarm and attacks fiercely, if in range.

If a major alarm is sounded (i.e. the party's intrusion is detected), Grimulak prepares for battle and enters the scene after 1d4+2 rounds. Should Grimulak be defeated, half the remaining ogres try to flee, while the other half retreat to the inner keep (**Area 15**) where they hope to better defend themselves.

Tactics: If you use this option, your party will face a much harder time getting into Durgam's Folly. The following tactics should lead to a success. These are given as examples. If your players come up with a different plan, you should let them try it. If you are certain the characters are going for a suicidal plan, you may wish to give them a hint or two that there may be better solutions.

• **The Trojan Horse Tactic.** The characters may try to convince Trina to hand over one of the caravan's wagons. The characters can hide inside the wagon and provoke an attack by the ogres. The coachmen then flee, and the wagon is taken inside the fort to be looted. Alternatively, one stealthy character might hide in the wagon and then try to find a way to open the gates for the remaining characters and caravan guards.

• **The Secret Tunnel.** This tactic requires using **Option 2: The Secret Tunnel** (see below) as well. Using this secret passage secures undetected entry into Durgam's Folly.

Once inside, the next task is to defeat more than two dozen ogres as well as Grimulak,

A Little Help, Please?

If your players are having serious trouble devising a good tactic to handle the situation, you may want to provide some helpful hints:

• **Create a Diversion!.** While the majority of the characters remains on top of the tower (**Area 5**) firing ranged attacks, one stealthy character might try to arm and free the prisoners held in the northeastern guard tower (**Area 9**). Just when the ogres recover from the shock of being under fire from above, the freed prisoners burst out to overwhelm them!

• **Signal the Attack!.** The party may also want to have the caravan guards move as close to the fort as possible, hide, and wait for a signal from them to start their attack (i.e. if they managed to open the gates.)

In any case, the party should try to make up a good strategy, either one of the above, a combination of all the above, or some other plan that might seem fitting and promises success with little losses. You should make it clear to all of your players that a straightforward attack without any strategic plan will most probably lead to their certain deaths.

Option 2: The Secret Tunnel

A secret passage enters Durgam's Folly. Thevik and Uli know about it and tell the characters where to find the entrance, if they are convinced that the characters are fully trustworthy. Neither Theodocious nor Trina is aware of this passage. None of the senior officers ever trusted the mage and his apprentice any farther than they can spit.

The entrance is about 2,000 yards southeast of the fort, hidden beneath a couple of bushes. A large, seemingly out-of-place monolith marks this colony of briars. To find the trapdoor, the briars must be cut or burned away. The latter is not a good idea, however, as the ogres in the southeast tower (**Area 5**) might spot the smoke. A round, iron trapdoor about three feet in diameter lies hidden beneath five inches of soil. A handle allows a character to lift it open. Below the trapdoor, a tube-like manhole of the same diameter as the door leads 30 feet straight into darkness. An old, rusted, iron ladder makes climbing down an easy task. Though the ladder looks badly damaged, it is sturdy and holds the weight of any adventurer. This manhole is too tight to allow more than one creature to climb into it at a time.

The manmade tunnel is roughly 2,000 yards long and only five feet in diameter. It is filled with stale water to a height of 3-1/2 feet. It leads to the basement of the southeast tower (**Area 5**) of the fort. The exiting manhole is identical to the entry shaft in all respects.

This was an old sewer that was never finished and subsequently forgotten by about everyone except for the fort's senior officers, who keep it as a secret flight passage. It descends slightly toward the center at 1,000 yards and ascends again afterward. At the tunnel's center, a crack in the wall allows the water to leak in.

The central 100 yards of the tunnel is completely underwater, which forces characters to dive and swim through. The characters may want to make sure it's passable by having the best swimmer explore the tunnel to find out. Point out that the characters must dive through the cramped tunnel in complete darkness with possible obstacles in their way (i.e. debris from parts of the ceiling that have collapsed, etc.). The entire tunnel is in a bad state of decay.

The tunnel allows characters an easier way to enter Durgam's Folly undetected, but also soaking wet and quite tired. Nevertheless, once inside the fort, the characters better have a good plan if **Option 1** is used!

• **Thunderstorms!** To further increase tension, you may wish to have a heavy thunderstorm come up. Once it starts raining, the water level in the tunnel starts rising rapidly, which should put the characters under substantial time constraints. The passage will be completely flooded within one hour after it starts raining and will be impossible to pass for at least three days unless the characters have some magical abilities. Three days is a long time for the ogres' captives in the fort …

• ***The Wight's Retreat.*** You still might want to add even more danger to this passage. Insert **Rainier the wight**, who is lurking in the tunnel. This poor soul is actually one of the men from the garrison who tried to flee from the murdering clockworks to find help. He drowned in the tunnel and, due to the presence of the nearby temple of Orcus, he rose as a wight only days later.

This passage is his lair, and he immediately attacks any intruders. Also, more of his comrades rot here. Currently, two male human corpses are here, one badly torn from a fall into the tunnel. Neither of the dead have risen as wights for some reason. Rainier leaves the tunnel at night to hunt and kill (he wants company). He always uses the exit outside Durgam's Folly. The wight's body is covered in scratches from the briars around the exit.

Note: Entering Durgam's Folly through this passage is pointless if **Option 1: Ogres on Guard!** is not used. Should you decide to leave the ogres off guard but add the tunnel anyway, I suggest you bring in Rainier the wight to make the tunnel a more dangerous encounter.

OPTION 3: USEFUL THINGS

Adventurers often find many useful things during their adventures. A *potion of gaseous form* may well save the day, while a magic weapon is one of an adventurer's basic needs. Some items are very different, however. They are vicious boobytraps.

But the brain gear thinks ahead, very much like a chess master. It figured that the ogres will not hold Durgam's Folly for too long, so it came up with a cunning idea.

To subdue more potent enemies such as experienced adventurers, it constructed a set of insidious tools as bait for intruders. It ordered Grimulak to place them in Theodocious' study (**Area 7**). These are intended to help the brain gear gather information about possible enemies.

When the party enters Theodocious' study, it is empty (as described in the adventure) except for a single supply crate. Its lid has been cracked open, and it is mostly empty. At the bottom of the crate are six identical metal boxes, each one five inches long, five inches wide, and one inch thick. They are wrapped in a soft cloth seemingly to prevent damage.

The surface of the boxes is slightly irregular and seems to be composed of small metal sticks about the size and shape of common matches. Embedded on the top of each box is a compass and a small lamp. The lamp can be turned on and off using a button on top. A small symbol resembling a stylized sun is to the right of each button. Experienced characters might find it suspicious that such useful items were simply abandoned. But this multi-functioning tool is a goodie an adventurer likely won't leave to rot. That's the catch. Each box is a dangerous device known as a **spymaker clockwork** (see sidebar).

Note: This option can be used independently from **Options 1** and **2**. Even if you decide to use them, you don't have to use this one. It's all up to you.

If you use the spymaker clockwork, the brain gear most likely knows what the characters are up to after one of them is injected with a thorn. It can send clockworks directly to their location in waves to stop them. The brain gear won't hesitate to electrify the thorns in implanted characters if they get too close to its inner sanctum where it is most vulnerable. You should carefully consider this before adding this option to the adventure.

SPYMAKER CLOCKWORK

Spymaker clockworks are mindless devices created by clockwork brain gears. The spymaker clockwork does not need to be in contact with a brain gear to function, however, and can operate even outside the normal two-mile range of most clockwork creations. They instead follow one programmed command.

If stored in a backpack, the spymaker detects body heat and burrows its way through the backpack on six retractable legs and attempts to pierce the victim's spinal cord with a retractable stinger (attacking as a 3 Hit Dice creature). If successful, it injects a tiny thorn and retracts the stinger, leaving behind the tiny thorn. The victim feels a slight pinch in the back, but unless this is investigated within one hour — during which time the entry wound is still visible — she or he will not notice anything. A thorn that is found can be successfully removed if another character makes a successful saving throw to pull it out. Failure causes the thorn to deliver a mild electrical shock for 1d6 points of damage to the implanted host.

Any character with an implanted spymaker's thorn could become an unwilling and unaware spy of the brain gear. Within three hours, each implanted target must make a saving throw or the brain gear is from then on able to see, hear, smell, taste, and feel everything the character does. This effect works to a distance of up to five miles from any brain gear.

Even worse, unwitting victims of the spymaker might not find out about the thorn in their spinal cord until they come within 30 feet of the brain gear. At this range, the brain gear can send a nasty electrical shock through the thorn that does 3d6 points of damage, or half that amount if the target makes a successful saving throw. The electrical discharge shorts out the thorn, robbing the brain gear of its spy.

While moving in a backpack, characters within 10 feet of the target have a 1-in-6 chance to notice the spymaker. The spymaker is loaded with up to a maximum of 12 thorns. If the last thorn is used, the spymaker ceases to function entirely. It cannot be repaired or reloaded.

Designation of Product Identity: The following items are hereby designated as Product Identity as provided in section 1(e) of the Open Game License: Any and all material or content that could be claimed as Product Identity pursuant to section 1(e), below, is hereby claimed as product identity, including but not limited to: **1.** The name "Frog God Games" as well as all logos and identifying marks of Frog God Games, LLC, including but not limited to the Frog God logo and the phrase "Adventures worth winning," as well as the trade dress of Frog God Games products; **2.** The product name "The Lost Lands," "The Siege of Durgam's Folly" as well as any and all Frog God Games product names referenced in the work; **3.** All artwork, illustration, graphic design, maps, and cartography, including any text contained within such artwork, illustration, maps or cartography; **4.** The proper names, personality, descriptions and/or motivations of all artifacts, characters, races, countries, geographic locations, plane or planes of existence, gods, deities, events, magic items, organizations and/or groups unique to this book, but not their stat blocks or other game mechanic descriptions (if any), and also excluding any such names when they are included in monster, spell or feat names. **5.** Any other content previously designated as Product Identity is hereby designated as Product Identity and is used with permission and/or pursuant to license.

This printing is done under version 1.0a of the Open Game License, below.

Notice of Open Game Content: This product contains Open Game Content, as defined in the Open Game License, below. Open Game Content may only be Used under and in terms of the Open Game License.

Designation of Open Game Content: Subject to the Product Identity Designation herein, the following material is designated as Open Game Content. (1) all monster statistics, descriptions of special abilities, and sentences including game mechanics such as die rolls, probabilities, and/or other material required to be open game content as part of the game rules, or previously released as Open Game Content, (2) all portions of spell descriptions that include rules-specific definitions of the effect of the spells, and all material previously released as Open Game Content, (3) all other descriptions of game-rule effects specifying die rolls or other mechanic features of the game, whether in traps, magic items, hazards, or anywhere else in the text, (4) all previously released Open Game Content, material required to be Open Game Content under the terms of the Open Game License, and public domain material anywhere in the text.

Use of Content from *The Tome of Horrors Complete*: This product contains or references content from *The Tome of Horrors Complete* and/or other monster *Tomes* by Frog God Games. Such content is used by permission and an abbreviated Section 15 entry has been approved. Citation to monsters from *The Tome of Horrors Complete* or other monster *Tomes* must be done by citation to that original work.

OPEN GAME LICENSE Version 1.0a The following text is the property of Wizards of the Coast, Inc. and is Copyright 2000 Wizards of the Coast, Inc. ("Wizards"). All Rights Reserved.

1. Definitions: (a) "Contributors" means the copyright and/or trademark owners who have contributed Open Game Content; (b) "Derivative Material" means copyrighted material including derivative works and translations (including into other computer languages), potation, modification, correction, addition, extension, upgrade, improvement, compilation, abridgment or other form in which an existing work may be recast, transformed or adapted; (c) "Distribute" means to reproduce, license, rent, lease, sell, broadcast, publicly display, transmit or otherwise distribute; (d) "Open Game Content" means the game mechanic and includes the methods, procedures, processes and routines to the extent such content does not embody the Product Identity and is an enhancement over the prior art and any additional content clearly identified as Open Game Content by the Contributor, and means any work covered by this License, including translations and derivative works under copyright law, but specifically excludes Product Identity; (e) "Product Identity" means product and product line names, logos and identifying marks including trade dress; artifacts; creatures; characters; stories, storylines, plots, thematic elements, dialogue, incidents, language, artwork, symbols, designs, depictions, likenesses, formats, poses, concepts, themes and graphic, photographic and other visual or audio representations; names and descriptions of characters, spells, enchantments, personalities, teams, personas, likenesses and special abilities; places, locations, environments, creatures, equipment, magical or supernatural abilities or effects, logos, symbols, or graphic designs; and any other trademark or registered trademark clearly identified as Product identity by the owner of the Product Identity, and which specifically excludes the Open Game Content; (f) "Trademark" means the logos, names, mark, sign, motto, designs that are used by a Contributor to identify itself or its products or the associated products contributed to the Open Game License by the Contributor; (g) "Use", "Used" or "Using" means to use, Distribute, copy, edit, format, modify, translate and otherwise create Derivative Material of Open Game Content; (h) "You" or "Your" means the licensee in terms of this agreement.

2. The License: This License applies to any Open Game Content that contains a notice indicating that the Open Game Content may only be Used under and in terms of this License. You must affix such a notice to any Open Game Content that you Use. No terms may be added to or subtracted from this License except as described by the License itself. No other terms or conditions may be applied to any Open Game Content distributed using this License.

3. Offer and Acceptance: By Using the Open Game Content You indicate Your acceptance of the terms of this License.

4. Grant and Consideration: In consideration for agreeing to use this License, the Contributors grant You a perpetual, worldwide, royalty-free, non-exclusive license with the exact terms of this License to Use, the Open Game Content.

5. Representation of Authority to Contribute: If You are contributing original material as Open Game Content, You represent that Your Contributions are Your original creation and/or You have sufficient rights to grant the rights conveyed by this License.

6. Notice of License Copyright: You must update the COPYRIGHT NOTICE portion of this License to include the exact text of the COPYRIGHT NOTICE of any Open Game Content You are copying, modifying or distributing, and You must add the title, the copyright date, and the copyright holder's name to the COPYRIGHT NOTICE of any original Open Game Content you Distribute.

7. Use of Product Identity: You agree not to Use any Product Identity, including as an indication as to compatibility, except as expressly licensed in another, independent Agreement with the owner of each element of that Product Identity. You agree not to indicate compatibility or co-adaptability with any Trademark or Registered Trademark in conjunction with a work containing Open Game Content except as expressly licensed in another, independent Agreement with the owner of such Trademark or Registered Trademark. The use of any Product Identity in Open Game Content does not constitute a challenge to the ownership of that Product Identity. The owner of any Product Identity used in Open Game Content shall retain all rights, title and interest in and to that Product Identity.

8. Identification: If you distribute Open Game Content You must clearly indicate which portions of the work that you are distributing are Open Game Content.

9. Updating the License: Wizards or its designated Agents may publish updated versions of this License. You may use any authorized version of this License to copy, modify and distribute any Open Game Content originally distributed under any version of this License.

10. Copy of this License: You MUST include a copy of this License with every copy of the Open Game Content You Distribute.

11. Use of Contributor Credits: You may not market or advertise the Open Game Content using the name of any Contributor unless You have written permission from the Contributor to do so.

12. Inability to Comply: If it is impossible for You to comply with any of the terms of this License with respect to some or all of the Open Game Content due to statute, judicial order, or governmental regulation then You may not Use any Open Game Material so affected.

13. Termination: This License will terminate automatically if You fail to comply with all terms herein and fail to cure such breach within 30 days of becoming aware of the breach. All sublicenses shall survive the termination of this License.

14. Reformation: If any provision of this License is held to be unenforceable, such provision shall be reformed only to the extent necessary to make it enforceable.

15. COPYRIGHT NOTICE

OOpen Game License v 1.0a Copyright 2000, Wizards of the Coast, Inc.

System Reference Document Copyright 2000, Wizards of the Coast, Inc.; Authors Jonathon Tweet, Monte Cook, Skip Williams, based on original mate-rial by E. Gary Gygax and Dave Arneson.

System Reference Document 5.0 Copyright 2016, Wizards of the Coast, Inc.; Authors Mike Mearls, Jeremy Crawford, Chris Perkins, Rodney Thompson, Peter Lee, James Wyatt, Robert J. Schwalb, Bruce R. Cordell, Chris Sims, and Steve Townshend, based on original material by E. Gary Gygax and Dave Arneson.

Swords & Wizardry Core Rules, Copyright 2008, Matthew J. Finch

Swords & Wizardry Complete Rules, Copyright 2010, Matthew J. Finch

The Tome of Horrors Complete. Copyright 2011, Necromancer Games, Inc., published and distributed by Frog God Games; Author Scott Greene, based on original material by Gary Gygax.

Tome of Horrors Swords & Wizardry Update © 2018, Frog God Games, LLC; Authors: Kevin Baase, Erica Balsley, John "Pexx" Barnhouse, Christopher Bishop, Casey Christofferson, Jim Collura, Andrea Costantini, Jayson 'Rocky' Gardner, Zach Glazar, Meghan Greene, Scott Greene, Lance Hawvermale, Travis Hawvermale, Ian S. Johnston, Bill Kenower, Patrick Lawinger, Rhiannon Louve, Ian McGarty, Edwin Nagy, James Patterson, Nathan Paul, Patrick N. Pilgrim, Clark Peterson, Anthony Pryor, Greg Ragland, Robert Schwalb, G. Scott Swift, Greg A. Vaughan, and Bill Webb.

The Siege of Durgam's Folly, © 2020, Frog God Games; Author Mike Mearls

www.ingramcontent.com/pod-product-compliance
Lightning Source LLC
Chambersburg PA
CBHW042012120726
47911CB00028B/833